"What happened?" Emma asked angrily.

"Did Diana tell you I was hot and heavy with Trent or something?"

"She didn't say that. She just pointed out that you and Trent had been going out for years and years," Kurt said.

"Oh, so that got you to thinking, is that it?" she said hotly. "You said to yourself, 'Gee, Emma lied to me before, so how can I trust her? And Diana did say she went out with Trent forever, and Diana is such a trustworthy human being—'"

"I'm really sorry, Emma. She just started me thinking. I told you it wouldn't matter to me—"

"You're a liar, Kurt Ackerman. If it really wouldn't matter to you, then you never would have brought it up," Emma said sadly.

The SUNSET ISLAND series
by Cherie Bennett

Sunset Island
Sunset Kiss
Sunset Dreams
Sunset Farewell

Sunset Farewell

CHERIE BENNETT

SPLASH™

B

A BERKLEY / SPLASH BOOK

SUNSET FAREWELL is an original publication
of The Berkley Publishing Group.
This work has never appeared before in book form.

A Berkley Book / published by arrangement with
General Licensing Company, Inc.

PRINTING HISTORY
Berkley edition / September 1991

A GLC BOOK

Splash is a trademark of General Licensing Company, Inc.

ISBN: 0-425-12772-9

A BERKLEY BOOK® TM 757,375
Berkley Books are published by The Berkley Publishing Group,
200 Madison Avenue, New York, New York 10016.
The name "BERKLEY" and the "B" logo
are trademarks belonging to Berkley Publishing Corporation.

PRINTED IN THE UNITED STATES OF AMERICA

10 9 8 7 6 5 4 3 2 1

As always, for Jeff
(Where did I find you?)

ONE

"Hey, lady, could I interest you in some very *private* private lessons?" Kurt Ackerman came up behind his girlfriend, Emma Cresswell, and whispered insinuatingly in her ear.

She turned around and faced him with a look of feigned innocence. "That would be swimming lessons, right?"

"That would be," he agreed, "unless you have something else in mind."

"Not me," she said, shaking her head.

"Ah, proper to the very end," Kurt said with a regretful sigh.

"Oh, really?" Emma said. She grabbed his T-shirt, pulled him to her, and kissed him hard. "There," she said, when she had left him completely breathless. "That was a seriously improper kiss."

"I'll say," Kurt managed.

The two of them were standing on the back porch of the Sunset Country Club, where Kurt worked as head swimming instructor. Because it was a rather cold day, they were completely alone, but they knew that someone could come out and catch them at any moment. Kissing while on duty was frowned upon for the staff.

Emma felt rather proud of herself. She had certainly come a long way since her arrival on Sunset Island. Had it really only been a few short weeks since she'd gotten off the ferry feeling totally unsure of herself and of what the summer might hold for her?

Emma thought back on her decision to take a job for the summer. As a Cresswell, of the Boston Cresswells, Emma had never worked a day in her life. In the rarefied atmosphere in which she lived—educated abroad, invited to all of the "right" functions with all of the "right" people—this was accepted behavior. But as Emma approached her senior year at Aubergame, her Swiss boarding school, she had started to see things differently. She was no longer satisfied to accept things the way they were. She didn't want to follow in the footsteps of her hypocritical, egocentric parents. There was a whole great big world out there, and Emma wanted to explore it.

She had decided to take a job as an au pair, and she'd been hired by Jane and Jeff Hewitt to care for their children at their summer home on Sunset Island, off the coast of Maine.

It had turned out well, actually. She liked the down-to-earth Hewitts and was becoming like a big sister to the kids. Emma had also made two great friends in Samantha Bridges and Carrie Alden, whom she had met at an au pair convention in New York. She even had her first really serious boyfriend. The only bad part of the experience was that she had lied to everybody at first about her background, not wanting them to know she was extremely rich for fear that they would treat her differently. Later, when her new friends found out the truth, they'd been angry with Emma for lying to them. Well, now that some time had passed, all of that anger was in the past. And she was delighted to find that scared, insecure, ever-so-proper Emma Cresswell had become confident enough to take Kurt Ackerman's breath away with a kiss on the back porch of the Sunset Country Club.

3

"I guess I'd better get back to the pool," Kurt said with a sigh, "much as I would rather stay out here and let you molest me."

"I'll molest you later," Emma said playfully. "How's that?"

"Promises, promises." Kurt checked his watch. "Oops, I gotta run."

"Okay. What time are you picking me up tonight?" Emma asked eagerly. Since Kurt was going to college and working two jobs, he rarely had an evening off. For over a week he and Emma had been planning a romantic picnic in the dunes.

"Eight-thirty or so," Kurt said.

Emma was disappointed. "I thought your last swimming lesson was at six."

"It was," Kurt said, "but Diana De Witt came by this morning and asked me if I could give her a private diving lesson at seven. That's the only time she's free."

Emma knew Diana De Witt only too well. They had gone all through school together in Switzerland, and they absolutely loathed each other. Emma had chosen her job on Sunset Island thinking that she would never run into anybody she knew there. But it turned out that Diana was a friend of another au pair, Lorell Courtland, who had invited Diana to spend some time on the island.

Since Diana's arrival she had done everything she could to make Emma's life miserable. She'd even gone out of her way to put Kurt down for being poor, and she had tried her best to break the two of them up. The fact that Kurt would change the time of their date to accommodate Diana De Witt just made Emma see red.

"We have to miss the sunset tonight because of Diana De Witt, of all people?" Emma picked up her beach bag and slung it over her shoulder.

"I told her no at first, but she really pleaded with me," Kurt explained. "She offered to pay double."

"Oh, so that makes it okay," Emma said coolly.

"Hey, I need the bucks, even if you don't," Kurt responded.

Emma immediately regretted coming down so hard on Kurt. He really did need the money. He was working his butt off to put himself through college. Sometimes she was thoughtless about money, since she'd never had to worry about it in her life.

"I'm sorry," Emma said softly, putting her

arms around Kurt's neck. "Eight-thirty is fine." She kissed him lightly on the lips.

"Will you wear your white bathing suit?" Kurt asked in a low voice.

"We're not going swimming," Emma pointed out.

"I know." Kurt gave her a grin that melted her heart, then waved and headed for the pool.

Emma smiled to herself as she walked into the game room to get the two older Hewitt kids. Tonight was going to be fabulous.

"Hi. You guys ready?" Emma asked, walking up to six-year-old Wills and eleven-year-old Ethan.

"I won an extra game," Ethan said, not taking his eyes off the video game in front of him.

"Great," Emma said. She sat down at a nearby table to wait for him.

Wills sat next to her. "Ethan always wins extra games," he complained. "I never do."

"Maybe that's because Ethan's older," Emma said, "so his reflexes are quicker or something."

"He always gets to be older." Wills sighed.

"I'm afraid that's true," Emma said, look-

6

ing at Will's dejected, freckled face. "But it won't matter so much later on," Emma promised. "In fact, when you're both grown up, it won't matter at all."

"I'll never be grown up," Wills decided, resting his chin on his hand.

"Oh, it'll happen," Emma assured him. She reached into her beach bag and pulled out a coin purse containing the money Jane had given her to spend on the kids. "Here," Emma said, handing Wills a dollar. "Go buy yourself something at the snack bar."

"Anything I want?" Wills asked. He obviously felt that he had to be sure, probably because Emma usually told him just what he could and could not have.

"Anything you want," Emma confirmed. "You decide."

Wills looked sideways at his big brother, who was totally absorbed in his game. "Does Ethan get a dollar, too?"

"Just you this time," Emma said softly. "Our secret."

"Thanks," Wills said, breaking into a grin that revealed his two missing front teeth.

Emma watched Wills race to the snack bar as her friend Sam waved to her from the doorway.

"Girlfriend!" Sam called, rushing over to Emma.

"Hi, Sam. Great bathing suit." Sam's acid green bikini with black piping looked terrific with her wild red hair.

"It's new," Sam confessed. "I spent much more for it than I should have. I was depressed. What can I say? Do you know what it's like spending days on end with the monsters trying to be the world's most perfect au pair?"

Sam was the au pair for thirteen-year-old identical twins Allie and Becky Jacobs. Recently Sam had almost lost her job when Mr. Jacobs found out she'd posed for modeling shots in see-through lingerie. Sam, who wanted desperately to be a model, had believed that the photos were only for her portfolio. Then to her horror she'd found out that the photographer, Flash Hathaway, had blown up the shots and exhibited them at a private club. Emma knew that what really made Sam angry was that she had known all along in her heart that she shouldn't trust Flash Hathaway, but she hadn't listened to her own best advice. Fortunately she'd been able to get the negatives back with the help of Jane Hewitt, who was a lawyer. Since that little scandal, though, she had bent over backwards to be perfect at her job, which meant spending all her time with the twins, and Emma knew that was torture for Sam.

"So tell me everything I've missed," Sam said, leaning forward eagerly.

Emma shrugged. "Not much. I have a date with Kurt tonight, and last night Carrie and I went to the Play Café to hear the Flirts. Carrie said you had to take the twins to a ball game."

"A ball game for twins, no less," Sam groaned. "Picture it—dozens of sets of identical twins in cutesy matching outfits, all playing baseball. It was a benefit for the local chapter of the National Twin Society. Their father just kept jumping around snapping pictures of them. You know the twins— they posed for their dad and then flirted with the coach, who is a college student."

Emma laughed. "Just the right age for them."

"So they think," Sam agreed, then sighed. "I was seriously bummed to miss the Flirts last night."

Flirting with Danger, or the Flirts, was the hottest band around. Carrie was getting hot and heavy with Billy Sampson, their lead singer. Sam had just started seeing the bass guitarist, Presley Travis.

"Was Kristy there?" Sam asked. She meant Kristy Powell, a wild girl of about twenty who lived on the island. Kristy had made it very clear that she wanted Presley and would do just about anything to get him.

"She was," Emma admitted, "but Pres didn't pay much attention to her."

"That's good," Sam said. "He hasn't called me, though," she added, "and for some reason I haven't called him, either. I'm in a wait-and-see mode, I guess. So what else is going on?"

"Did I mention that I have a date with Kurt tonight?"

"Yep," Sam confirmed.

"Oh," Emma said. "Aren't you going to ask me about it?"

Sam laughed and pushed her red hair out of her face. "Gee, Emma, what do you and Kurt plan to do on your date tonight?" she asked innocently.

Emma leaned forward. "Can you keep a secret?" she asked eagerly.

"Is the pope Catholic?" Sam answered.

"Well," Emma whispered, "I think tonight's the night."

Sam looked confused. "The night for what?"

"You know," Emma whispered. *"The night."*

The light finally dawned. "You mean you and Kurt are going to finally *do it?*" Sam practically screamed.

"Shhh!" Emma hissed, looking around to see if anyone had heard Sam. "Honestly, why don't you just grab a mike and broadcast it over the P.A. system?"

"Okay," Sam said, "but I warn you, spectators may show up to witness the event."

"Very amusing," Emma muttered.

"It's just that no one believes that girls as beautiful as you actually have sex," Sam explained. "We just assume that you're the product of an immaculate conception and that your children will be, too."

"Well, I'm so happy I decided to confide in you," Emma said, pushing her chair away from the table.

"All right! Another free game!" Ethan yelled.

"Come on," Sam said, stopping Emma. "I'm sorry. I'll curb my levity, okay?"

"My love life is nothing to laugh at," Emma said.

"I'll say," Sam agreed.

Sam looked so serious that Emma burst out laughing.

"Ah, Ms. Cresswell locates her sense of humor," Sam said with a grin. "Seriously, this is big news," she added. "So when did you two decide?"

"We didn't, exactly."

"You mean you decided and Kurt doesn't know?"

"Something like that," Emma admitted.

"Whoa, girl, don't you think this should be, like, a mutual decision?" Sam asked.

"Well, Kurt's been ready since our second date," Emma confessed. "I'm the one who insisted on waiting. I've always wanted my first time to be . . . special. And I needed to make sure that Kurt was special enough for me to want to be with him."

"And you've decided he is?" Sam asked.

"Don't you think he's wonderful?" Emma sighed.

"Yeah, a great guy," Sam agreed.

"And don't you think it will be a wonderful experience?"

"How would I know?" Sam asked. "I'm probably the oldest living virgin in America."

"Nuns are often older," Emma pointed out with a laugh.

"Just don't let it get around that I'm as pure as the driven snow," Sam begged. "My reputation would be ruined."

Wills came running over to the table carrying a half-eaten double-dip chocolate ice cream cone. "Hi, Sam," he said between slurps.

"Hi, Wills. The ice cream looks great."

"It is," Wills agreed, happily licking the cone and covering his face with chocolate. He wandered over to watch his brother's video game, clearly hoping that Ethan would notice his ice cream cone.

"Let me ask you a question," Emma whispered to Sam when she was sure Wills was out of earshot. "Do you think I should actually say something to Kurt, or should I just, you know, not stop him?"

"I think you should show up for your date wrapped in cellophane and yell 'surprise!' He'll get the idea."

"Sam!"

"Okay, okay. What I really think is that you and Kurt should discuss it. This is a big decision."

"Won't talking about it make it less romantic?" Emma asked.

"Depends on how you handle it, I guess," Sam said. "Just make sure he knows it's a decision you made and that you're not just carried away or something stupid like that. And make sure you plan for this, if you catch my drift."

Emma nervously twisted a strand of straight blond hair around her finger. "You mean go into a drugstore and buy . . . protection?" Emma asked tentatively, making a face.

"Prophylactics," Sam enunciated. "Rubbers."

"Sam!" Emma cried. "Someone will hear you!"

"So what?" Sam shook her head. "It's not a dirty word, you know. Even a real lady like you is allowed to utter it."

"God, I'll die of embarrassment if I have to ask for condoms," Emma whispered.

"You could die if you don't," Sam pointed out.

Emma sighed. "This doesn't sound very romantic anymore."

"Sorry," Sam said. "This is life in the nineties. Anyway, it'll be as romantic as you guys want it to be."

"What will?" Wills asked, gulping down the last of his ice cream cone.

14

"Wills!" Emma said. "I didn't realize you were standing there! How much of that conversation did you hear?"

"The part about someone could die and then the romance part," Wills said, wiping a chocolate-smeared hand across his face.

"Go wash off the ice cream, okay?" Emma said, pointing to the men's room.

"Yeah, yeah, yeah," Willis said. "I suppose you're gonna tell me I'm too young to know what you guys were talking about."

"You suppose right," Emma said.

"Couldn't you just pretend I'm already an adult?" Wills asked hopefully. "After all, you're the one who told me it's only a matter of time."

"Go wash," Emma said.

"It's not fair," Wills muttered as he dragged his feet to the men's room.

"That is a very cute kid," Sam said.

"I'm just glad he didn't hear more," Emma said with a shudder. "I didn't even realize he was standing there."

"That's because you were too busy picturing Kurt's naked hunky body, muscles rippling in the moonlight as he wraps his manly arms around your—"

"Sam!"

Sam laughed and jumped out of her chair.

15

"Gotta run, babe. The twins await. Listen, if I may be serioso for a moment, have a wonderful time tonight. I hope it turns out to be everything that you want it to be."

"Thanks, Sam," Emma said, smiling at her friend.

"And I want to hear every detail!"

"Dream on!" Emma laughed. "This is one moment of my summer that is not open for discussion."

TWO

By eight-fifteen Emma was totally prepared for her date with Kurt and was pacing her room on the third floor of the Hewitts' house. She checked her appearance in the mirror one more time, not sure she had chosen the right outfit. What did a girl wear to lose her virginity in, anyway?

She stared at her reflection. "'Lose her virginity.' Stupid expression," Emma muttered. She straightened the shoulders of her pink and white striped T-shirt and checked the waistband of her pale pink cotton miniskirt. *Cute outfit. Easy to take off*, she thought, blushing at her own audacity.

No, Emma told herself firmly. *I'm a grown-up. I'm taking responsibility for planning this, and that's good.* She pictured the gorgeous lingerie she was wearing un-

17

derneath her simple outfit. Her lacy white teddy was made of the finest, sheerest silk imported from Paris. Although Emma had decided to leave behind in Boston her expensive designer wardrobe and buy the kind of casual, inexpensive clothes that all the girls wore on the island, she hadn't left behind her hand-stitched French lingerie. Thinking about the momentous evening' she had planned, she was glad.

At eight-thirty Emma nervously checked her purse for the purchase she'd made that afternoon. At first she'd been horribly embarrassed. She'd circled the block five times before she finally worked up the nerve to go into the drugstore. And then she'd picked up twenty items she didn't need before adding that tiny, all-important box to her purchases. The young girl ringing up the purchases hadn't even blinked an eye.

Yep, there was that small box, nestled in the bottom of her purse. So far so good. But how could she tell Kurt about it or suggest that he use one or—God forbid—have to figure out how to get it out of the box and on him? What if he didn't know how, either? She shuddered at the thought and told herself that everything would work out—she hoped.

18

Emma jumped when she heard the phone ring and guiltily snapped her purse shut as if someone could see her.

"Emma! Phone!" Jane yelled up the stairs.

"Thanks," Emma yelled back, picking up the extension on the nightstand.

"Hi, it's Carrie. I wanted to wish you luck tonight."

Emma sighed. "I suppose Sam told you."

"Wasn't I supposed to know?" Carrie asked.

"It's just that I specifically told her not to tell anyone," Emma said. "I didn't mean you, of course," she added quickly. "I would have told you myself. It's just the principle of the thing."

"I'm sure she wouldn't tell anyone but me," Carrie assured her.

"I hope not." Emma sounded doubtful.

"Anyway, I'm happy for you," Carrie said. "I think Kurt's terrific."

"Yeah, he is," Emma said with a small smile. "I'm just so nervous. Is that normal?"

"Well, from my great wealth of experience, which is to say one guy, I can only tell you that I wasn't nervous at all. But then, I'd been going steady with Josh for three years by that time."

19

"So maybe I'm rushing this," Emma said, twisting the phone cord around her finger.

"I didn't mean that."

"But what do you think?" Emma pressed. Carrie was so smart and level-headed; Emma really valued her opinion.

"I think it's a very personal, individual decision," Carrie said. "As long as you're doing it for the right reasons, it should be fine."

"Well, how do I know if I'm doing it for the right reasons? What are the right reasons, anyway?"

"Well, because you really want to, I guess, and not because someone else wants you to," Carrie said. "Gee, I just realized I'm talking to myself as much as to you," she added with a laugh. "That probably means you should ignore me completely."

"No, no, you're right," Emma said. "You'll figure out what to do with Billy."

"Hey, Emma, Kurt's here!" Wills screamed upstairs.

"Oh, my God, Carrie, he's here," Emma breathed into the phone.

"It's not an execution," Carrie pointed out with a laugh. "Go have a wonderful time."

Emma grabbed her purse and ran down

20

the two flights of stairs. Three-year-old Katie was standing in the foyer holding Kurt's hand. He was her swimming teacher, and she was madly in love with him.

"Kurt came to see me and Sally," Katie told Emma happily. Sally, Katie's favorite doll, was always clasped in whichever hand was free.

"How's my second-favorite girl?" Kurt asked Emma with a grin.

"I see that women of all ages throw themselves at you," Emma told Kurt with a slightly raised eyebrow.

Kurt shrugged and grinned. "They just can't help themselves."

God, he looked darling in his faded jeans and a blue and white cotton shirt with the short sleeves rolled up to show his tanned, muscular arms. Emma just had to grin back at him.

"Are you going out with Emma?" Katie asked, looking up at Kurt. "Can I come?"

"Not this time, sweetie," Kurt told her. "But how about if we take you to the beach sometime soon?"

"When?" Katie asked practically. "Today is Wednesday, so we could go tomorrow. Tomorrow is Thursday."

Jane Hewitt walked in from the den and overheard her daughter. "Boy, you can tell this kid has lawyers for parents," she said with a laugh. "She's already learned the fine arts of specificity and negotiation."

"How about Saturday?" Kurt suggested. "That's three days away."

"I know." Katie was very proud of having recently learned the days of the week and how to count to one hundred. She repeated both feats endlessly for anyone who would listen. "Three days away is very far," she added solemnly.

"Oh, I think the time will go past quickly," Emma said, stooping to hug the little girl.

"Come on, helper, it's time to bake cookies," Jane told her daughter. Katie went eagerly. Cookie baking took precedence over everything, even Kurt.

"Thrown over for a batch of chocolate chip cookies." Kurt sighed as he and Emma got into his car.

"You'll get over it," Emma said, patting his knee. She opened the window on her side of the car and let the cool night breeze rush past her face. "Mmm, the air here smells so great," she said. "Salty and sweet at the same time."

Kurt smiled without taking his eyes off the road. He had grown up on Sunset Island, as had three generations of his family before him. There was nothing he loved more than knowing that Emma appreciated the beauty of his home.

"Did I mention that you look particularly darling tonight?" Kurt asked Emma as he made a right turn and headed for the dunes.

"Even though I didn't wear my white bathing suit?" Emma teased.

"You would look hot in a shower curtain," Kurt told her. "Preferably a see-through one," he added playfully.

Emma remembered Sam advising her to wrap herself in cellophane for this date, and she laughed. "You're not the first person to suggest something like that," she said.

"Don't tell me—it was that guy, what's-his-name," Kurt said with a scowl.

"What guy are you talking about? It wasn't a guy at all," Emma said. "It was Sam making a joke. You know Sam."

"I thought maybe it was that Trent guy, your old boyfriend," Kurt said, pulling up near the dunes and turning off the engine.

"I told you before, he wasn't my boyfriend," Emma said as they got out of the car. It was the truth. Trent Hayden-Bishop III was the son of friends of Emma's parents, and she'd been paired up with him for everything from her first dance lessons to her coming-out party. But she'd never cared about him the way she cared about Kurt, and she'd certainly never lusted after him the way she lusted after Kurt.

"That's not what Diana said." Kurt popped open the trunk of his car to get out an old blanket and spread it on the sand.

His comment made Emma so angry that for a second she couldn't even speak. Diana had invited Trent to Sunset Island without Emma's knowledge and then had brought him to a party the Hewitts gave, knowing that Emma had a date with Kurt. Kurt had shown up at the party just as a semi-drunk Trent was grabbing at Emma. Diana and her obnoxious friends had gleefully told Kurt that Trent was Emma's boyfriend. Emma hadn't yet had a chance to tell Kurt about Trent, so even though Trent wasn't really her boyfriend, Kurt had been upset. Diana had set the whole thing up, and here Kurt was quoting Diana as if he actually believed her!

"I got champagne," Kurt said, showing

Emma a bottle and two plastic champagne glasses he'd hidden in the trunk.

Emma gave him a tight smile, but waited until the two of them were seated on the blanket before saying, "Listen, Kurt, Diana is the last person you should ever believe about anything—particularly anything concerning me," she said.

Kurt worked on the cork of the champagne bottle. "I didn't say I believed her. I just told you what she said." The cork popped, and Kurt poured two glasses of the bubbly liquid. "To us," he said softly, lightly clinking his plastic glass against Emma's.

She smiled, more sincerely this time, and took a sip of the champagne, but his comment was still nagging at her. "I guess I just don't know why you repeated it," Emma said. "Why were you and Diana talking about Trent and me, anyway?"

"The subject just happened to come up," Kurt said. "You don't need to make a big deal out of it."

"I'm not making a big deal out of it," Emma said. She took another sip of her champagne. "How did it 'just come up,' if I might ask?"

"I was asking her what you were like

when you were a girl, if you really want to know."

"Oh, great," Emma muttered. "She probably told you I was a serial killer. Why on earth would you ask her that?"

Kurt gave Emma a strange look. "I asked her because I happen to be crazy about you, and because I'm crazy about you I'm interested in everything about you, and she's the only person I know who knew you as a kid, okay?"

"So what horrible things did she say about me?" Emma asked.

Kurt took a long drink of his champagne. "Actually, she said you were always beautiful and you never went through an awkward stage. She said she used to put every chemical in the world on her hair, trying to get it to look like yours."

"She said that?" Emma asked, shocked.

"She did," Kurt confirmed. "She also said you were always very, very ladylike, and you were really into being rich."

"It figures she'd throw a zinger in there," Emma said. "I was not really into being rich. I never even thought about it."

"Why doesn't that surprise me?" Kurt murmured.

Emma's wealth was a sore point between them. Maybe it wouldn't have been so bad if Emma had told Kurt right away that her family was one of the richest in the country. But Kurt was proud and he could be a bit stiff-necked, so it might have been difficult anyway.

"I don't want to fight," Emma said softly, putting her hand on Kurt's arm. "I think it was sweet that you wanted to know what I was like as a girl," she said. *And I'll be damned if I'll let Diana De Witt ruin this night for me*, she added silently.

"I don't want to fight, either," Kurt said, kissing Emma lightly on the lips. "Mmm, you taste like champagne," he whispered.

"So do you," she said, licking his lips lightly.

Kurt gently pressed Emma down on the blanket. He dipped one finger into her champagne and softly drew a line from her ear down her throat. Then he gently licked the trail of champagne off her skin.

It was exquisite. Emma closed her eyes and felt Kurt's warm breath on her skin. Again he kissed the trail of champagne, and his kisses continued down the V-neck of her top. Her arms went around him as he

27

pressed his lips to hers. Time seemed to stop, and Emma floated in a state of bliss, growing more and more excited. *I should tell him now,* she thought, *just open my mouth and tell him I've decided, and not just let it happen or make him guess.* But every time Emma tried to get the words out, Kurt's kisses stopped her, and everything felt so perfect that she didn't want to endanger what promised to be the most wonderful evening of her life.

Kurt tenderly raised Emma up enough to pull off her shirt. He kissed his way down her neck, slowly slipping the narrow silk strap of her teddy from her shoulder. He did the same on the other side until the top of her teddy fell to her waist. He sat back and looked at her. "You are so beautiful," he murmured huskily.

Kurt unbuttoned his shirt and pressed his bare chest against her. When his hand moved under her skirt and she didn't stop him, Emma could feel his surprise. She knew she should tell him that tonight was the night, that she had prepared for it. This had to be the right time. But what if it wasn't? What if her timing made everything awful and they both got awkward and self-conscious? No. She wouldn't let herself think that way. Sam was right about her taking responsibility. Now was the time to assert herself and—

"Emma?"

"What?"

"Are you sure?" Kurt asked. They had never gone this far before. "I know how much this means to you."

"Well, doesn't it mean as much to you?" Emma whispered.

"Yes, it's very, very special," Kurt said in a low voice. "But it's even more special for you."

"Why is it more special for me?" Emma asked nervously. She wanted it to mean everything in the world to him to make love to her.

"Because you said it would be your first time," Kurt explained patiently.

"What do you mean, 'I *said* it would be my first time'? It will be my first time."

"Well, I just wondered . . ." Kurt began.

Emma sat up and covered herself with his shirt. "You wondered what?" she asked.

"Nothing. It doesn't matter," Kurt said hastily.

"It *does* matter," Emma insisted.

"I just meant that I know you lied to me in the past about a few things, and I don't want you to feel you have to lie about this, because it wouldn't make any difference in my feelings for you."

"Well, aren't you a wonderful human being?" Emma said sarcastically.

"Look, that didn't come out the way I meant it—" Kurt began.

"First of all, I *was* telling you the truth, and second of all, it wouldn't really be any of your business if I wasn't telling you the truth, and third of all, you are acting like a jerk!"

"You're right," Kurt said. "I'm sorry. Can't we just forget it?"

"No, we can't." Emma said, pulling her teddy up and dropping her shirt over her head. How could this be happening? Everything had been so wonderful, so perfect. Now Kurt was ruining everything! "I can't believe you said what you said," Emma said, hugging her chest miserably.

"Aren't you overreacting a little?" Kurt asked. "I told you I don't care."

"If you don't care, why did you bring it up?" Emma shot back. "The truth is you *do* care, and you don't trust me. What happened? Did Diana tell you I slept with Trent or something?"

"She didn't say that. She just pointed out that you and Trent had been going out for years and years," Kurt said.

"Oh, so that got you to thinking, is that it?" she said hotly. "You said to yourself, 'Gee, Emma lied to me before, so how can I trust her? And Diana did say she went out with Trent forever, and Diana is such a trustworthy human being—'"

"I'm really sorry, Emma. She just started me thinking. I told you it wouldn't matter to me—"

"You're a liar, Kurt Ackerman. If it really wouldn't matter to you, then you never would have brought it up," Emma said sadly. "You notice I never asked you."

"I would have told you," Kurt said. "That's the point."

"No, the point is that if we really love each other, the past shouldn't be relevant at all," Emma said. "Besides, I did tell you, but you don't believe me because of something Diana said to you."

"It wasn't like that," Kurt said. "We were just talking—"

"Oh, sure, Kurt," Emma interrupted. "You just don't understand anything!"

31

"That's not true." Kurt ran one hand through his hair. "It's—it's . . . hard to know what's real with you, that's all," he said softly.

Emma stood up with tears in her eyes. "I'd like to slap that pious look right off your face."

Kurt stood up, too. "Please, Emma, don't be like this." He reached for her arm.

Emma shook him off. "I hate you for ruining this for me!" she cried passionately. She wiped the tears from her cheek with the back of her hand. "I want to go home."

They didn't speak on the way back to the Hewitts'. Kurt parked in the driveway and turned to Emma.

"Emma, I'm really sorry. Please believe me."

"Why should I believe you? You obviously don't believe me when I tell you things," Emma pointed out.

"Ouch," Kurt said, wincing. "I guess I deserved that." He ran his hand through his hair, something he often did when he was upset. "I really messed this one up, didn't I?"

Emma nodded, but she refused to look at him.

"I acted like a jerk."

Emma nodded again.

"I'll make it up to you," Kurt promised. "Sometimes I . . . I guess I just get kind of insecure about you."

"But you have nothing to be insecure about!" Emma cried.

"I'll try to keep that in mind," Kurt said wryly, reaching over to touch her hair. "Did I really ruin everything?"

"Yes."

There was silence in the car. She looked over at him, the moonlight outlining the fear etched on his face. His beautiful face. The face she loved.

"For tonight," she finally added.

"Oh, Emma," he said softly, then took her in his arms.

Moments later Emma let herself into the house and climbed slowly up to her room. She lay down on her bed and thought about the tiny box that still lay, unopened and unneeded, in the bottom of her purse.

And she wasn't sure if she was sort of sorry, sort of glad, or sort of both.

THREE

Emma felt glum and out of sorts the next day. She hated fighting with Kurt. She played their argument over and over in her mind. Maybe it hadn't been completely his fault. In the light of day she didn't feel certain about anything.

"I'm off to take Katie to her swimming lesson," Jeff Hewitt said, coming into the kitchen where Emma was unloading the dishwasher. "Is Ethan all packed?"

The older boy was leaving on a camping trip with his Boy Scout troop. He was incredibly excited and had chattered with Emma all morning while she helped him fill his backpack. Emma was glad Ethan could talk with her easily now. Not too long ago he'd had such a mad crush on her that he could barely carry on a conversation in her presence. That seemed to have passed, maybe because Audrey Sheppard, a cute girl from the country club had become his girlfriend. She was twelve—an older woman—and she sometimes called Ethan up, giggled, and then hung up the phone.

"Yes, he's packed," Emma said, standing on tiptoe to put the glasses away. Sometimes she wished she were taller than five feet five. It would be so much more convenient. "Stuey Stein and his dad are supposed to pick Ethan up in an hour. He's already waiting out in front."

Jeff Hewitt smiled. "I remember my first long camping trip with my friends. It was a very big deal. As I recall, some kid told a ghost story that was so scary we all slept with our flashlights on."

Jane had taken Wills with her to Bangor as a special treat, since he was so jealous over Ethan's camping trip. Katie stayed with her dad after Ethan left, and so Emma found herself with no responsibilities and no plans. She decided to run up to her room, throw on some shorts, and go jogging on the beach. Maybe that would help clear last night's fiasco from her mind.

"Yo, anyone home?" Emma heard someone yelling from the front porch as she was tying her sneakers. She ran to a hall window and saw Sam and Carrie looking up at her.

"Hi!" Emma called. "I'll be right down." She grabbed her beach bag and ran down the stairs. "I didn't expect to see you two."

"You know us, impetuous youth," Sam said, pushing her sunglasses up into her hair. "Besides, the twins are with Daddy Dearest at a seminar called Family Communications. That ought to be a riot."

"And Claudia took the kids to her mom's in Greenwich overnight, so I have the whole day free," Carrie said happily.

Carrie was the au pair for Graham and Claudia Templeton. She hadn't had a clue when she'd been hired by the Templetons' family manager that Graham Templeton was actually rock superstar Graham Perry. Graham was back out on the road, and Claudia was spending a lot of time with her two kids.

"We're going out to lunch. Can you come with us?" Carrie added.

"As a matter of fact, I can," Emma said. "Everyone's out. I was just about to go jogging on the beach."

Sam looked at Emma's white cotton

shorts, white Lycra top, and white sneakers. "You have on no makeup and you're dressed to jog, and you still look perfect. It's nauseating."

Emma laughed. Earlier in the summer she might have taken offense, but she had learned that Sam didn't mean anything by her blunt comments. "What can I say? I'm walking perfection," Emma said lightly. "Let's go."

A few minutes later, after they had settled around their favorite table at the Play Café and placed their orders, Emma realized that Carrie and Sam were staring at her.

"What?" she asked.

"You know very well what," Sam said.

"Last night?" Carrie prompted. "You don't have to tell us anything if you don't want to."

"Yes, she does," Sam told Carrie. "It says so in the teenage girls' handbook. We're supposed to tell each other everything. If nothing good happens, we're supposed to make something up."

"Well, then, I guess I'll have to make something up," Emma said with a sigh, "because nothing good happened."

"Did you change your mind?" Carrie asked. "That's okay."

37

"I didn't change my mind," Emma said. "Just . . . oh, I don't know what happened. Everything was awful. We had this huge fight."

Emma related the conversation she'd had with Kurt the night before, and told her friends how it had escalated into an argument.

"So that's about it," she concluded. "We made up at the end, sort of. But I still feel terrible about it."

"So you think Diana De Witt set you up on purpose?" Carrie asked.

"Let's rename her Diana De Bitch," Sam suggested, "a name that really fits her. Of *course* she did it on purpose. She's trying to break them up."

"Two cheeseburgers deluxe, one spinach salad, three ice teas," the waitress said as she set down their food.

"Eat half my fries," Carrie told Sam, putting a handful on Sam's plate. Sam was known for her gargantuan appetite, and Carrie was always watching her weight.

Emma picked at her salad and then put her fork down. "The thing that really upsets me is that Kurt listens to her and doesn't trust me," Emma said unhappily.

"Well, you did lie to him before," Carrie pointed out.

"That's what he said," Emma said glumly.

"That's a stupid reason," Sam said between bites of her burger. "If you love someone, you have to trust them," Sam pronounced.

"I agree," Carrie said. "I'm just saying it might take Kurt some time to trust Emma because of what happened before. Besides, like you said, it shouldn't make any difference to him if you did sleep with Trent. It's not relevant to your relationship with him in any way."

"All guys are like that," Sam said, swallowing a fry. "They think they have a right to know your entire personal history. Of course if you tell them, they get all weirded out."

"Kurt's not like all guys," Emma said. Or was he? Maybe she didn't know him as well as she thought she did. Suddenly she wasn't hungry at all.

"Don't look now, but Ms. De Bitch and her buddies just walked in the door," Sam announced.

Emma turned to look. Sure enough, there was Diana with Lorell and Daphne. Diana, a smug grin on her face, was heading for their table.

"Oh, great," Emma muttered, turning back to her friends. "I really need this."

"Well, if it isn't the Three Musketeers," Lorell sang out. Lorell was from Atlanta, and her exaggerated nasal drawl did real harm to the image of southern belles everywhere.

"Lorell, your dulcet tones are a real appetite killer," Sam said, putting down her burger.

Lorell put her hand lightly on the back of Carrie's chair and leaned over her. "I bet you wish I affected you that way," she said. Carrie blanched at the comment. Although she had a sexy, curvaceous figure, Carrie felt self-conscious about it and tended to cover up with baggy clothing. Next to super-slim girls like Lorell, Carrie always felt fat.

"Confidentially," Lorell continued in Carrie's ear, "horizontal stripes are not a good choice for a girl with your, um, type of figure."

Carrie dropped the french fry that was halfway to her mouth and bit her lower lip. She was wearing an oversize red and white striped t-shirt over baggy red shorts. When she'd put it on she thought it looked cute and comfortable. Now she was certain she looked like a house.

"Carrie looks great," Emma said, defending her friend.

"I was only tryin' to help!" Lorell drawled, wide-eyed.

"Lorell is very helpful when it comes to fashion," Diana agreed.

"Yeah, helpful," Daphne echoed. Daphne Whittinger was Lorell's lackey, constantly hanging over her and doing whatever Lorell told her to do. Daphne always seemed nervous, hyper, and unhappy. She was also excruciatingly thin, but seemed to think she was fat. Emma and her friends suspected that something was seriously wrong with the girl.

Diana sat down uninvited in the fourth chair at their table. She leaned forward chummily and spoke to Emma. "I'll tell you how helpful Lorell is. She helped me pick out the new bathing suit I wore yesterday for my private diving lesson with your boyfriend."

"How kind of her," Emma said frostily.

"Well, that's just the sort of friend she is," Diana agreed. "It's the cutest suit—hot pink

41

with an underwire bra top—you know, the kind that gives you unbelievable cleavage." Diana looked at Emma's smallish bustline. "Well, it gives *me* unbelievable cleavage, anyway. I was a little concerned that I might just pop out of the top! Now, wouldn't that have been embarrassing?"

Emma just stared at her. It was patently obvious that Diana wouldn't have found top-lessness at all embarrassing.

"Anyway, you'll be glad to know that didn't happen," Diana assured Emma. "What with Kurt standing there with his arms around me to correct my form, it could have made for a tense moment!"

"What say we blow this pop stand?" Sam said, throwing down her napkin in disgust.

"You know," Lorell said, "you ladies—and I use the term loosely—really need to learn something about manners."

"Oh, we do know about manners," Emma assured her, standing up. "That's why we're leaving before we say things we might regret."

"Speaking of things you might regret, I have another private lesson with Aquaman tonight," Diana told Emma. "Just thought you might be interested."

"Nothing about you interests me," Emma said coolly, walking away from the table. Sam and Carrie followed close behind.

"Ooh, tough comeback," Lorell crooned.

"Bye-bye!" Daphne called, waving at the girls as they walked to the cash register. "Stay in touch!"

They paid quickly and walked out into the afternoon sunshine.

"What is wrong with them?" Sam exploded. "Those girls are seriously disturbed!"

"Do I look really fat in this?" Carrie asked her friends.

"No, of course not. Please don't let her get to you," Emma said. "Girls like Lorell and Diana just love to undermine your confidence. They think if they make you weaker, they'll seem stronger. So they pick at whatever you feel most insecure about," Emma explained.

Sam looked at Emma with admiration. "Well put, compadre. How did you get so smart?"

"Oh, believe me, I've known girls like that all my life." Emma sighed. "I don't know what makes them so mean. Maybe their lives are so narrow and insulated that superficial things become meaningful to them, or something. How you look is more important to them than the kind of person you are. Things like that."

"Meaning I really do look fat in this, but I'm a nice person?" Carrie asked as they got into Claudia Templeton's Porsche.

"Carrie," Sam said, "for a babe who's going to Yale in the fall, you are not demonstrating your alleged brain power."

"I know," Carrie said. "I know how stupid I sound. Sometimes I think my self-confidence is a mile wide and an inch thick." She expertly turned the Porsche around a corner and headed for the Hewitts' house.

"Well, join the club," Sam said.

"Do you really think she has another private lesson with Kurt?" Emma asked her friends.

"I wouldn't put it past her," Sam said. "I used to think Diana De Bitch was out to get you. Now I think she's out to get your guy."

Carrie pulled into the Hewitts' driveway and stopped the car.

"But why would she want Kurt?" Emma asked. "It doesn't make any sense. He's poor. Diana would never go out with a guy who's poor."

"Maybe she just wants him because you have him," Carrie suggested.

"Why does she hate me so much?" Emma asked.

Neither of her friends could supply her with an answer that made any sense.

FOUR

Emma didn't hear from Kurt all day. His silence nagged at the back of her mind, filling her with anxiety. If he was so sorry about what he'd said, why hadn't he called her?

After dinner Emma finally had time to take her jog on the beach. She ran long and hard, trying to clear her mind. When she reached the pier she dropped to the sand and stared out at the endless ocean. In the distance she could see a huge yacht silhouetted by the setting sun. For a moment she wished she were aboard that yacht, sailing away from Sunset Island, away from responsibilities and guy troubles. Then she smiled to herself, because she realized that if she really wanted to sail off on a yacht just like that, all she had to do was pack up and

46

go. No one was forcing her to stay in Maine and play "responsible Emma." No one but herself, that is.

Half an hour later when Emma got back to the house, she saw a midnight blue Lotus she didn't recognize in the driveway. Wills was in front of the house playing catch with a skinny older boy wearing a Mets T-shirt.

"This is Dougie," Wills said importantly, introducing his friend. "His family moved in next door to Stinky. He's ten," Wills added, obviously proud to be playing with an older kid. Stinky Stein was Wills's best friend, who lived next door. No one seemed to know Stinky's real first name, not even his parents.

"Hi, Dougie," Emma said, pulling the sweatband off her hair. She turned back to Wills. "Nice car. Who does it belong to?"

Wills shrugged and threw the ball to Dougie. "Some guy looking for you. He's inside with Mom and Dad."

"For me?" Emma asked in surprise. She couldn't imagine who it could be.

"Well, hi there, long time no see," a lazy voice greeted her as she walked into the Hewitts' family room. Sitting in the easy chair talking to Jeff and Jane was Trent Hayden-Bishop III. The last time Emma

47

had seen him he was mauling her at the Hewitts' party. She'd been completely disgusted with him. She certainly hadn't expected him to return to Sunset Island.

"Trent," she said in what she hoped was a civil tone. "This is unexpected."

"Trent was telling us about the sailboat he just bought," Jane said. "He's planning to race it."

Trent grinned. "I named her *The Split*, after a stock that did."

"We'll leave you two alone," Jeff said, getting up from the couch. "Jane and I are off to the movies, Emma. We'll be back around eleven. Nice to see you again, Trent," he added as he and his wife headed for the door.

"I'm surprised the Hewitts were so civil to you, since the only time they met you was when you got drunk at their party and made a huge scene," Emma said, sitting on the couch.

"I apologized profusely," Trent said. "I simply explained how distraught I was to find that you were in love with someone else."

"You were distraught for maybe five seconds," Emma said, "and Jeff and Jane are too smart to buy that story."

48

"You underestimate my charm," Trent said with a grin, shaking his head so that a lock of brown hair would fall forward on his forehead and he could push it back. It was a studied gesture Emma had seen many times. Even his clothes were studied— white flannel pleated pants, a white silk T-shirt, and a navy blazer that Emma knew had been hand-tailored for him in England. She used to think he dressed great. Now his outfit just looked overdone and pretentious to her.

"What are you doing here?" Emma asked, pushing her blond hair back behind one ear.

"I came to see you," Trent said innocently.

"No, you didn't," Emma said.

"I came to show off my new Lotus?" Trent asked.

Emma laughed. "That sounds more like you."

"Let's go for a spin," Trent suggested, getting up.

"I can't. I'm working, remember? I promised Katie I'd read her a story before bed."

"Oh, come on, Emma, anyone can read the kid a story," Trent said. "Read her one tomorrow night."

"Don't you get it? This is my job! These

49

kids are my responsibility!" Emma was really annoyed now. "Contrary to what you may think, the world does not revolve around you and your every desire."

"I recall a time when you were interested in my every desire," Trent insinuated.

"Don't pretend our relationship was something it wasn't," Emma snapped. "Listen, I need to take a shower, and then I have to give Katie her bath. I've got work to do."

"Which is your less than subtle way of telling me to get lost," Trent said.

"Something like that," Emma agreed.

"Emma, Emma, Emma," Trent chided her. "You used to be the best-mannered girl I knew. Now you take a job and put on this droll little-poor-girl act, and your manners get shot to hell."

"Which is exactly where you can go, Trent," Emma said, turning on her heel to leave.

"Hey, come back! I'm sorry!" Trent said with laughter in his voice. "You've become quite the feisty one of late. It suits you."

Emma opened her mouth to make a quick retort, but Trent stopped her.

"I'll stop sparring if you will," he said,

holding his palms up in a peace gesture. "Truce?"

Emma stared at him a moment, remembering that they'd been friends of a sort all her life. She had no reason to be defensive around him. It wasn't as if he could drag her back to being the person she used to be.

"Okay, truce," she finally said with a small smile. "Now will you tell me what you're really doing here?"

"Actually, I had fun the last time—once I got over you, that is," Trent added solemnly. "Diana called me last week to tell me that the house next door to the Popes—where Lorell's staying—is vacant now. The owner is a playwright, and his show is having some kind of trouble back in New York, so he had to split. I decided to rent it from him. It's a great house," he added.

Emma could hardly believe what she'd just heard. "You rented a house on the island?"

"I can tell you're overcome with enthusiasm," Trent said with a grin.

"It's just . . . I just—" Emma stammered. She didn't know what to say. She had chosen to work on Sunset Island because she was so certain no one she knew

51

would be there. Then her stepfather-to-be, twenty-five-year-old Austin Payne, had shown up for an exhibit at the local gallery. Later, Lorell had invited Diana De Witt to the island, and she'd stayed on as Daphne's houseguest. Now Trent was renting a house! The island was overrun with people from her past! How could she become an entirely new person when ghosts from her old life kept haunting her new one?

"I don't plan to cramp your style with lover boy, if that's your big concern," Trent said.

"His name is Kurt," Emma snapped.

"Touchy, touchy," Trent said. "Listen, I'm not planning to give you a bad time with him. And just to show you there are no hard feelings, I'm giving a party tomorrow night, and I want you to invite him. I'll apologize to him in person. How's that?"

"Actually, that would be very nice," Emma said, surprised at Trent's largess.

"Come around eight. Invite all your friends," Trent said, slipping on his eight hundred dollar sunglasses. "It's the white house on the cliff at the end of Beach Road." He kissed Emma lightly on the lips and touched a fingertip to her slightly sunburned nose. "I was distraught for a lot longer than five seconds, you know," he said softly. Then he ambled out to his Lotus.

Maybe it would be okay that Trent was here, Emma thought later, as she jumped into a steaming hot shower. Maybe it would do Kurt good to see that another guy thought she was special. Not that she'd flirt with Trent or anything. She absolutely would not play that game. But after the way Kurt had acted, he could use a little low-level competition.

"Hey, Emma, can I go to the beach with Dougie tomorrow?" Wills asked Emma as she was tucking Katie into bed.

"Sure," Emma said, opening Katie's favorite book, *The Cat in the Hat.*

"Dougie is ten, you know," Wills said, leaning on the wall of Katie's bedroom.

"That's almost as old as Ethan," Katie said. "One, two, three, four, five, six, seven, eight, nine, ten, eleven!" she finished proudly.

"Yeah, but he's my friend," Wills pointed out, "not Ethan's."

"Twelve, thirteen, fourteen . . ." Katie continued.

Wills beat a hasty retreat. He was obviously tired of hearing his little sister count.

Katie was asleep before Emma finished reading the book. She looked so sweet that Emma reached down and kissed the top of her head. What would it be like to have a little girl of her own? she wondered. *Right, Emma,* she told herself. *You're barely learning how to handle being a parents' helper, much less being a parent!*

The phone rang just as Emma was about to go up to her room. She picked it up in the hall.

"Hi, it's me," came Kurt's deep voice.

"Hi," Emma said carefully. She was glad to hear from him, but she wanted to wait and see what his attitude would be.

"I just got home from the club," Kurt said. "I wanted to call you right away. You still mad at me?"

"No, not really," Emma said softly. How could she stay mad at him when she was so crazy about him?

"I thought about things," Kurt continued, "and I was a jerk. Everything just got out of hand."

"That's what I think, too," Emma said eagerly.

"So do we get to try again?" Kurt asked, his low voice sending shivers up her spine.

"Try what?" she asked flirtatiously.

"You know very well what," Kurt said. "I couldn't sleep last night. I kept thinking about how beautiful you looked," he breathed into the phone.

"That's so sweet," Emma whispered.

"When can I see you?"

"Want to come to a party with me tomorrow night?" Emma asked him.

"Yeah, I actually have the night off," Kurt said. "Where?"

"Don't get the wrong idea about this," Emma began, "but Trent has the house next door to the Popes, where Lorell allegedly works, and he's giving a party tomorrow night."

"Trent!" Kurt exploded. "What the hell is he doing here on the island?"

"He likes it here," Emma said lamely.

"I'm not going to any party he's giving," Kurt fumed.

"Listen, before this turns into a fight, let me tell you that he specifically asked me to invite you," Emma said quickly. "He knows we're together. He wants to apologize to you for acting like such an ass the last time he was here."

"He does, huh?"

"He does," Emma confirmed. "Now, are you going to be a big enough person to let him?"

Silence. "Okay," Kurt finally relented.

"Good," Emma said with relief. "It'll be fun. He told me to invite my friends. I'll invite Sam and Carrie, and they can bring Pres and Billy."

"Will we get to be alone at all?" Kurt asked.

"Why would you want to be alone with me?" Emma asked innocently.

"I'd rather show you than tell you," Kurt said huskily.

"Well, I guess I could spare you a minute or two," Emma teased.

They arranged that Kurt would pick Emma up at eight the next night, and they said their good-byes. Emma hung up feeling much better about everything. Last night everything had just been blown out of proportion. So what if Kurt was a little jealous, even a little unreasonable sometimes? She wasn't perfect, either.

Emma ran up to her room and sat on the window seat looking out at the twinkling stars. Maybe tomorrow night would be the night. She pictured herself dancing with

Kurt at the party. Then they would leave early to go to their very favorite private spot in the dunes. Kurt would tell her he loved her, and he'd cherish her just as she longed to be cherished. Everything would be perfect, she just knew it. Now that Kurt had called and everything was great between them again, nothing could stand in her way.

FIVE

"You don't think this is going to cause problems?" Carrie asked Emma on the phone the next morning. Emma had just invited Carrie to Trent's party and had told her she was going with Kurt.

"I'm telling you that Trent wants to apologize to Kurt," Emma repeated.

"But Kurt is already suspicious about Trent. It just seems like playing with fire."

"But it isn't!" Emma insisted. "Look at it this way. The whole thing could work in my favor. Maybe when Kurt sees me around Trent, he'll realize there's absolutely nothing between us and he won't be suspicious anymore."

"Maybe," Carrie said, but she didn't sound convinced.

Emma laughed. "You worry even more than I do. How about if we just have fun?"

"You talked me into it," Carrie said. "And I can invite Billy?"

"Sure. Trent said to invite everyone, so pass the word around." Emma told Carrie which house Trent had rented.

"Wow, I know that house," Carrie said. "It looks sensational from the outside. I took Chloe near there to visit a little girl from her play group. I can't believe an eighteen-year-old guy can afford to rent it all by himself."

"Carrie, Trent could afford to *buy* it all by himself," Emma said mildly.

Carrie laughed. "Don't tell Sam. She'll decide he should be the father of her children."

"I already called and invited her," Emma said. "She's inviting Pres. I don't think Trent would stand a chance against that southern drawl of his."

"Not to mention those southern muscles of his!" Carrie added. "See you tonight!"

Just as Emma hung up the phone, it rang again.

"Hewitt residence," Emma said.

"Emma darling, it's your mother."

"Oh, hi," Emma said, a bit taken aback. It

was unusual for Emma's mother to call her. Generally speaking, Katerina Cresswell—or Kat, as she liked to be called—was much too involved in her own life to spend much time thinking about Emma's.

"How are you, darling?"

"I'm okay," Emma said. "Is everything all right?"

"Of course everything is all right," Kat said. "Can't a woman call her only child simply because she misses her?"

"Yes, a woman could," Emma agreed. "I'm just surprised you did."

Kat sighed into the phone. "I'm going to ignore that. Have you heard from your father?"

Now, that was a really odd question. Emma's parents were in the midst of an endless and ugly divorce. They spoke to each other only through lawyers. Emma's mother desperately wanted her freedom so that she could marry Austin Payne, but Emma's father was contesting the divorce. Kat and Austin had broken up when Kat found out that Austin was cheating on her with every young girl in sight, but the breakup had lasted only three weeks. As usual, Kat saw only what Kat wanted to see. Emma found the whole thing excruciating.

"No, I haven't," Emma said. "Why would I hear from daddy?"

"Because he's your father. Isn't that a good enough reason?" Kat said. "Honestly, Emma, you can be the most exasperating child."

"Well, I haven't heard from Daddy," Emma said. "Next question."

"Don't be rude, Emma," Kat said imperiously. "And don't think I haven't noticed that you call me Mother and you call him Daddy."

"Somehow 'Mommy' doesn't fit you, Mother," Emma said evenly.

"So call me Kat. It's about time, I think. We're both adults. Besides, you know no one believes I'm old enough to have an eighteen-year-old daughter," Kat added playfully.

"And yet you are," Emma pointed out. She couldn't help it. Her mother just brought out her bitchy side. However, after she was nasty she always felt guilty, so she couldn't win.

"Yes, I suppose I am," Kat said in a small voice. "I'm getting these terrible lines around my eyes."

Emma sighed. It always got to her when Kat turned things around and acted hurt.

"Mother, you're still incredibly beautiful. Everyone thinks so," Emma said reassuringly.

"Evidently your father doesn't," Kat said.

Emma was confused. "Pardon me?"

"Your father is dating a younger woman," Kat said darkly. "A much younger woman."

"Well, you're dating a much younger man," Emma pointed out.

"That is beside the point," Kat said. "This child your father's seeing is twenty-two years old, and he claims he's serious about her. In fact, they may become engaged. In other words, he is ready to negotiate the divorce at long last."

Emma was dumbstruck. Her father was practically engaged to some twenty-two-year-old girl she had never even heard about, much less met? And he was actually ready to stop contesting the divorce after all the years of fighting?

"Who . . . who is she?" Emma managed to say.

"Her name is Valerie," Kat said, spitting out the name like bad food. "I saw her picture. She bleaches her hair. She has fat ankles."

"Oh."

"I was much better looking at twenty-two, but your father has evidently decided I'm over the hill," Kat said.

"Uh-huh," Emma said.

"Don't say 'uh-huh,' Emma. It's not even a word." Kat sighed once again. "Well, I do think your father could have had the good grace to inform you that he's practically engaged."

"Maybe he'll call me," Emma said lamely.

"I doubt it. Your father was always too busy for you. But don't feel bad, darling. He was always too busy for me, too."

"Yes, well, I have to go now, Mother," Emma said. She felt the beginnings of a terrible headache right between her eyes.

"Just one more thing," Kat said. "I've decided to have a little medical procedure done, and I'll be in the hospital for a couple of days."

Emma's heart began to beat alarmingly fast. She didn't get along with her mother, but Kat was still the only mother she had. "Are you sick? Are you having surgery?"

"No to the first question, yes to the second. I'm going in for a little nip and tuck, that's all. Around the eyes and the chin. Don't you think it will do wonders?"

Kat had always resisted cosmetic surgery, claiming she looked so young that everyone thought she'd already had a face-lift.

"I think that's great," Emma said.

"Do you think I look old and I need a face-lift?" Kat asked sharply.

Now it was Emma's turn to sigh. Sometimes you just could not win with her mother. "I just meant if a face-lift will make you happy, then it's fine."

"Well, your father is chasing twenty-two-year-olds!"

"Mother, you haven't been interested in Daddy for years," Emma pointed out.

"Emma dear, you have a great deal to learn," Kat said frostily. "It is one thing for me not to want your father, and quite another thing for your father not to want me."

After saying good-bye to her mother, Emma wandered downstairs to see if Katie needed help changing into her bathing suit for her swimming lesson. She felt as if she were in a daze. Both her father and her mother might marry people young enough to be friends of hers. It was very creepy.

Emma followed the sound of a child's laughter to the back deck, where she found Jane tickling Katie, who was squealing with delight.

"I'm the tickle monster!" Jane growled, her fingers heading for Katie's pudgy little stomach.

"No! You're Mommy!" Katie squealed, throwing her arms around her mother's neck. Jane proceeded to cover her daughter with kisses.

For just a moment Emma felt her throat constrict. Had Kat ever tickled her and covered her with kisses? Not that Emma could remember. The closest her own mother had come to that was straightening the ribbon in Emma's hair when it wasn't perfect. A dim memory came to her, unbidden, of trying to climb on her mother's lap to kiss her. Kat had pushed her away, yelling for Nanny to please keep the child away from her when she was getting ready to go out. Her mother had looked so angry that she'd scared Emma, who had cried before her nanny could whisk her away. . . .

". . . and you can go to the beach with Wills and his friend, okay?" Jane said.

"Pardon me?" Emma was startled out of her reverie.

"I said I'll take Katie to swim class, and you can go with Wills and his new friend to the beach, if that's okay with you," Jane repeated.

65

"Oh, sure, fine."

"Today is Friday," Katie piped up. "Tomorrow is Saturday."

"That's right," Emma said, smiling at the little girl.

"Tomorrow Kurt is taking me to the beach," Katie said importantly. "He said Saturday."

Jane laughed. "Nothing gets past this kid," she said, hugging her daughter.

"You can come, too, Emma," Katie said.

Emma laughed. "Why, thank you, madam. You are too, too kind."

Katie giggled at the funny way Emma was talking. A butterfly caught her attention, and she pushed out of her mother's arms and toddled off after it.

"Tell me she isn't the cutest child on the planet," Jane said, looking fondly after her daughter.

"You won't get any argument from me," Emma said with a smile. "Where's Wills?"

"He's upstairs getting his stuff together for the beach. He's extremely excited to have made this new friend. The idea of hanging out with a ten-year-old is just the coolest thing in the world to him."

"Yes, he's casually mentioned to me at

66

least a dozen times that Dougie is ten," Emma said. "I'll just go get my beach stuff and see if Wills needs any help," she added, heading for the house.

"Oh, by the way, some old friends of ours called a little while ago. They're going to be on the island tonight," Jane said, "and we're meeting them for dinner at Victor's around seven. We should be home, say, ten-ish," Jane said.

"Oh, fine," Emma said quietly.

"That doesn't sound fine," Jane said. "Did you have plans?"

"A party," Emma said, "but I'll go late, that's all."

"I'm sorry not to have given you more notice," Jane said. "This dinner engagement came up unexpectedly."

"It's okay, really," Emma assured her. She headed upstairs to find Wills. This was Great. Just great. She couldn't very well object to the short notice—it was very unusual for Jane not to tell her well in advance if she and Jeff were going out. And caring for the kids was, after all, Emma's job. She'd just have to call Kurt and tell him they'd have to go to the party late. One more opportunity for their big night would be shot to hell.

"I'm all ready for the beach!" Wills yelled enthusiastically when Emma found him in his room. He had on his blue bathing trunks and his snorkel and fins. Emma bit back her laughter; it was bad enough that Ethan always teased Wills about wearing his snorkel and fins when he wasn't in the water. "Dougie's supposed to be here at eleven," Wills added, checking the time on his very first waterproof Day-Glo multicolored watch. "It's ten-forty now."

"Why don't you wait for him on the porch?" Emma suggested. "I'll just go change into my bathing suit and grab my stuff."

Emma pulled on her most modest bathing suit and threw a pair of shorts over it. She looked up Kurt's phone number in her address book. She might just catch him before he left for the club.

"Hello?" came Kurt's voice.

"Hi, it's me," Emma said softly.

"Hello, me," Kurt answered easily. "Nice to hear your voice before a hard day underwater. What's up?"

"Bad news," Emma said. "The Hewitts are going out tonight, so I have to work until ten."

"What a drag! How can they just change their schedule without giving you more notice?" Kurt sounded annoyed.

"They usually tell me way ahead of time," Emma said, "but some friends are coming to the island unexpectedly, so—"

"I'm kind of bummed," Kurt said. "You know how seldom I have an entire night off. And I have an eight o'clock class tomorrow morning. I can't party till dawn, much as I'd like to."

"I'm disappointed, too," Emma said. "Some evenings were not meant to be rushed," she added in a low voice.

"You have my wholehearted agreement on that," Kurt said huskily. "I can't wait to see you."

Kurt was being sweet, and Emma was sorry to spoil one of his few evenings off, so she seized an idea that suddenly popped into her head. "Listen, why don't you go to the party at eight, and I'll meet you there as soon as I can?" Emma suggested.

"No way!" Kurt said.

"Why not? There's no reason for you to sit at home for two hours when you could be dancing and having fun," Emma reasoned. "I'll feel better if I know you're not missing out on my account."

"Yeah, but it's Trent's party," Kurt said. "It'd be too weird going there without you."

"Actually, I think it would be good," Emma said, pacing with the phone. "The more I think about it, the more I think it makes sense."

"You do, huh?" Kurt teased.

"I really do. I'm sure Trent wants to apologize to you in private, anyway. This will give him a chance. And you know how crazy parties get later on."

"In other words you want me to catch the guy while he's still sober." Kurt laughed. "Okay, I'll go. But I want to see your beautiful self there ASAP. It won't be fun without you."

Emma hung up feeling she'd done the right thing. It would be good for Trent and Kurt to meet without her in the middle. And there really was no reason for Kurt to miss all the fun. Then, too, Trent thought the world of Emma and might tell Kurt how absolutely terrific she was, and that wouldn't hurt, either.

When Emma hit the front porch, Wills was nowhere to be found. "Wills!" she called.

"Coming!" he yelled from the basement.

Emma sat down on the steps. She couldn't

stop thinking about the party and about telling Kurt to go by himself. It wasn't a couples-only party, Emma told herself as she pulled her sunglasses out of her beach bag. Kurt would have fun. Everyone he knew on the island would probably be there.

Emma started to retie her sneaker, but stopped as a terrible thought hit her: Everyone Kurt knew on the island probably would be there, and that meant Diana. Diana and Kurt.

"That's ridiculous," Emma said out loud, standing up to stretch. After all, no matter how much Diana might want Kurt, he could never be interested in a snotty rich girl who referred to him derisively as Aquaman. Besides, Kurt loved her. And that was all the security that Emma needed.

SIX

"Does my hair look stupid like this?" Sam asked Emma, pushing her hair back on one side. They were in Emma's room waiting for Jeff and Jane to return home so they could leave for Trent's party. Sam had called Emma late in the afternoon and told her Pres had a cold and couldn't come to party. They had decided that Sam would come over to the Hewitts' and go to the party with Emma.

Katie had fallen asleep during her bedtime story, but Wills had taken forever to settle down. Sam didn't help. She introduced him to charades, and she kept imitating his favorite TV characters, which he thought was the funniest thing in the world. He begged her to do just one more and then just one more, until finally Emma had to

72

insist that Sam do the very last one while Wills was actually in bed, right before they turned off his light.

Now Sam was trying various hairstyles while Emma changed for the party. "Not stupid," Emma decided, "but it looked better before."

Emma studied the clothes in her closet and tried to decide what to wear. Sam shook her hair loose and joined Emma at the closet. "I'd go for simple and virginal," Sam advised. "That should remind Kurt of what he has not yet experienced with the beauteous Ms. Cresswell, which should really fire him up. Imagination is everything," she said knowingly.

"You're terrible." Emma laughed, selecting a white pleated cotton miniskirt and a white lace T-shirt with a sweetheart neckline.

"Ah, white," Sam sighed. "The color of girlish innocence."

She had on her favorite jeans, a white sleeveless men's T-shirt without a bra, and a wild-looking multicolored oversize jacket with huge padded shoulders. Naturally she was wearing red cowboy boots, her trademark.

"Not everyone can dress with your abandon," Emma said, slipping on the skirt and T-shirt.

"Oh, everyone can try, but few can pull it off." Sam studied her outfit in the mirror. "This jacket is excellent," she added, admiring her reflection, "even if I did blow a bundle on it."

"Aren't you supposed to be saving money for college?" Emma reminded her as she slipped on her white sandals.

"College, ugh!" Sam fell back on Emma's bed. "Honestly, from my parents' attitude you'd think a dance scholarship to Kansas State was like winning the Nobel Peace Prize or something."

"They're proud of you," Emma said as she brushed mascara on her eyelashes. "That's nice."

Sam sighed. "Oh, I guess, but I really, really do not want to go to college. Someone like Carrie now, she belongs in college."

"So where does someone like you belong?" Emma asked.

"Wine tasting in Paris with the rich and famous?" Sam suggested.

"I've done it," Emma said. "It's not so great."

"Listen, Emma, what say we trade lives?" Sam said, sitting up. "You go live with my family in our old farmhouse in Junction—the plumbing is always on the fritz, by the way—and I'll take the Concorde to Paris and hobnob with your millionaire buddies, okay?"

Emma laughed. "It would be worth it just to see the look on my mother's face when you showed up in that jacket."

They heard Jane and Jeff come into the house, so they grabbed their purses and ran down the two flights of stairs.

"Oh, hi, Sam," Jane said as she stashed her purse in the closet. "Great jacket."

"See? Some mothers have taste," Sam told Emma coolly.

"Everything okay with the kids?" Jeff asked.

"Fine," Emma said. "Wills is sleeping with his swim fins on. I really could not get them off him. Oh, and Dougie's mother called and invited Wills to go with their family on a picnic tomorrow," Emma added. "Their phone number is on the pad in the kitchen."

"Well, that was nice of her," Jane said.

"Wills is thrilled," Emma reported. "He told me that Dougie is the most grown-up friend he's ever had. Also the nicest and the smartest and the best at baseball."

"I just hope Dougie doesn't drop Wills when he gets to know more kids on the island—you know, kids closer to his age," Jeff said with a frown.

"Wills is so smart," Emma said. "He's not like an ordinary six-year-old. I think he can keep up just fine."

Jane gave Emma a little hug. "I knew there was a reason I liked you." She threw Emma the keys to the BMW. "Have fun tonight." She waved as the girls went outside.

"She doesn't know just how much fun," Sam said, wiggling her eyebrows insinuatingly at Emma as they got into the car.

"Uh-uh," Emma said. "This not going to be the night. Not enough time."

"From what I've heard, it doesn't take hours—that is, unless you get really, really lucky," Sam said.

"Very funny," Emma said, expertly pulling the car out of the driveway. "I just don't want it to be rushed. Everything has to be romantic and perfect."

"Did it ever occur to you that probably nothing Kurt could do or plan could live up to your expectations?" Sam asked.

Emma smiled. "When you've got the perfect guy, I believe the first time with him can be perfect."

Sam didn't answer. She just shrugged and stuck her head out the window to catch the breeze.

They could hear the loud bass line of a Graham Perry CD blaring out of an excellent sound system before they even turned into the long driveway to the house Trent had rented. There were so many cars parked in the drive that Emma had to leave the BMW down near the turnoff.

"Hmmm, this joint is jumping," Sam said as they walked to the house. A girl neither of them knew was laughing as two guys chased her around the outside of the house. She appeared to be wearing nothing more than a towel.

They climbed the four steps and made their way around two intertwined bodies before they realized it was Carrie and Billy Sampson.

"Hey, don't you two ever come up for air?" Sam asked when she realized she had almost stepped on Carrie.

"Hi!" Carrie said, grinning at her friends. "How long have you guys been here?"

Sam looked at Emma. "She is living proof that sex makes your IQ fall a good twenty points."

Emma nudged Sam in the ribs. She was glad that Carrie was so happy. It couldn't have happened to a nicer girl. "We just got here," she said. "I had to work late. Having fun?" She looked from Carrie's glowing face to Billy's dazed expression. "Silly question," she murmured.

"Hey, Pres was sorry he couldn't make it," Billy told Sam. Billy, Pres, and the other Flirts all lived together in a rented house in a slightly run-down section of the island. "He really sounded awful when I left, coughing and sneezing all over the place," Billy added. "We've got an important gig tomorrow night in Bangor, so he's got to get better." He looked lovingly at Carrie. "If he doesn't, I'll have to teach my girl here to play the bass real quick."

"Sorry, I'll be too busy taking pictures," Carrie told him. She was an excellent photographer and planned to become a photojournalist. She'd taken some backstage shots of Flirting with Danger and Graham Perry at a recent concert, and she'd sent the pictures off to a major rock magazine. She hadn't heard from them yet, but her hopes were high.

"Yeah?" Billy said playfully. "Would it be too much to ask you to put your camera down long enough to listen when I dedicate my new song to you?"

"Billy wrote a new song called 'Carrie,'" Carrie told her friends shyly. "I haven't heard it yet. He's going to sing it tomorrow night in Bangor."

"Yeah, and think about it," Billy said. "If we break up all I have to do is change the name just a little bit—Mary, Sherry—"

Carrie swatted his arm, but he caught her hand and pulled her to him for another kiss.

"And she's supposed to be the prim and proper one," Sam muttered as she and Emma walked into the house.

Trent was crossing the room with a bottle of champagne in either hand when he saw Emma and Sam come in.

"Fashionably late, I see," Trent said, kissing Emma lightly on the lips.

"This is my friend Sam Bridges," Emma told Trent. "Sam, this is Trent Hayden-Bishop."

Trent grinned at Sam. "You definitely do not look like a Sam, Sam," he told her.

"I take it that's a compliment," Sam said.

"You take it correctly," Trent agreed. "Are you a model or something like that?"

"Something like that," Sam said with a mysterious smile.

Emma definitely did not like the vibes going on between Trent and Sam. Trent was completely ignoring her! "I guess Kurt told you I had to work late," she said a bit too loud.

Trent tore his gaze away from Sam. "He did. We had quite the man-to-man talk," he sad with mock seriousness.

"You apologized?" Emma asked.

Trent nodded. "I was both honest and humble. . . . In other words, I lied."

Emma put her hands on her hips. "Trent, what did you say?"

"Relax. I told him you and I were definitely past tense. I also told him I was bombed at the Hewitts' party and that the always cool Emma Cresswell did not encourage me in any way."

This time is was Emma's turn to kiss Trent. "Thank you, Trent. That was very nice of you."

"Hey, what are old friends for?" Trent's gaze returned to Sam. "You like champagne?"

"I like good champagne," Sam said coolly.

"Then you're in luck," Trent said. He held out two bottles of Moët & Chandon for her inspection.

"Nice," Sam said in her most noncommittal voice, since she had no idea how to tell good champagne from bad.

Trent took Sam by the hand and started to lead her away. Then he turned back to Emma. "Oh, Kurt is in there somewhere." He waved vaguely with a champagne bottle at the living room, which was teeming with party guests.

Before Emma could make her way through the bodies to find Kurt, Lorell Courtland pranced up to her with a drink in her hand.

"Hey there, Emma, aren't you just cute as a button in that little outfit?" Lorell's singsong voice dripped sarcasm and rose shrilly over the blaring rock music. "I can't help but notice that mixin' with the cheap and tacky is startin' to affect your fashion sense. I thought you'd want to know," she added, wide-eyed.

Lorell, as usual, was impeccably dressed in designer originals. Her jade green raw silk T-shirt and pants fit her perfectly.

Emma leaned close to Lorell and spoke confidentially. "Thanks for the tip, Lorell. But some of us are confident enough not to have to wear our fortunes on our backs all the time."

"And some of us are tryin' desperately to be something we are not," Lorell retorted.

"Get a life, Lorell," Emma said, walking away. It had felt very good to say that. Usually she felt that Lorell's bitchiness got the best of her. Emma smiled to herself as she worked her way through the crowd. She hoped that some of Sam's audacity was rubbing off on her.

Once Emma had worked her way past the outer ring of people standing around talking—shouting, actually—over the music, she reached the center of the room where people were dancing. The first person she noticed was Daphne Whittinger, who was dancing wildly with Kip, a hunky lifeguard from the club. Daphne looked even thinner and sicker than she had when Emma had seen her just yesterday. Daphne wore a sleeveless black T-shirt with black jeans. Her arms stuck out of the shirt like match sticks. The hollows in her cheeks and the circles under her eyes gave her a haunted look. As Emma watched her dancing madly, she saw Daphne reach up to push her hair out of her face. To Emma's horror, a handful of hair came out in Daphne's hand. She hid it in her palm and then dropped it behind her back. No one else seemed to notice. Emma shivered, even though the room was warm. Surely she wasn't the only one who could see that this girl was seriously ill. *Well, it's none of my business*, she said to herself. She knew she was about the last person on the island from whom Daphne would ever accept help.

As Emma craned her neck to see if Kurt was among the dancers, the song ended. A flash of brilliant light caught Emma's eye. It was a diamond tennis bracelet on the slender wrist of Diana De Witt, as she swung her arm around Kurt's neck to give him a hug. Kurt was hugging her back. And Kurt was not letting go. Emma marched right up to them.

"Oh, hi, Emma," Diana said, her arms still draped around the neck of Emma's boyfriend. "Don't you look cute." Diana spoke in the same sarcastic tone as Lorell, minus the southern accent.

Emma had to admit that Diana looked

wonderful in a royal blue off-the-shoulder minidress that fit her like a second skin and showed off her terrific figure and golden tan to perfection. Her chestnut curls were tousled from dancing, and her blue eyes looked huge and catlike. Emma wanted to kill her.

"Hi," Kurt said, extricating himself from Diana's embrace. "I'm glad you're here," he added with a smile.

"Really? I never would have known," Emma said, looking pointedly at Diana and then back to Kurt.

"We were dancing," Kurt said, as if that wasn't obvious.

"So I see," Emma said coolly.

"I'm going to find a drink," Diana said, holding her hair off her neck and fanning herself. "See you," she added seductively to Kurt, then sauntered away.

The music started again.

"Dance?" Kurt said, holding his hands out to Emma.

"My party spirit seems to have deflated," Emma spat out.

"Come on, Em, what's wrong?" Kurt reached for her arm, but she shook him off and glared at him. This time he grabbed her arm and propelled her toward a long hall, where he opened the first door he found. "Okay, now, what's the problem?" Kurt asked, leading her into a bedroom and folding his arms in front of him.

"What's the problem?" Emma echoed. "I get stuck working late, and when I finally show up at the party there you are with Diana De Bitch's arms wrapped around your neck!"

"It's called dancing," Kurt said.

Emma put her hands on her hips. "Don't insult my intelligence."

Kurt ran a hand through his hair and sat down on the bed. "Let's discuss this calmly. You are blowing everything out of proportion."

Emma sat down next to him. "Well, then, enlighten me," she said frostily.

"Look, you told me to come early and have fun, remember? It wasn't my idea! I would gladly have waited for you."

"I told you to come early so you wouldn't miss the fun," Emma interrupted, "not so that you could dance with Diana!"

"Sorry, Emma, but you can't tell me which girls I can dance with," Kurt said evenly.

"Don't you get it?" Emma asked. "She is making a play for you, and she's only doing it because she hates me. She has no interest in you!"

A muscle twitched in Kurt's cheek. "Is it so impossible to believe she might like me?"

"No, of course not!" Emma cried. "But Diana isn't like that! She's the cruelest, most manipulative witch I've ever met, with the possible exception of her bosom buddy, Lorell."

"She's really not that bad, Em. Maybe she's grown up since you knew her at school."

"Oh, spare me." Emma jumped up to pace the room. "School only ended a couple of months ago. Believe me, I'm wise to all her tricks."

"Well, she speaks highly of you," Kurt said mildly.

"That's part of her plan!" Emma twirled around to face Kurt. "She says nice things about me so that she'll look good!" Emma sat down again next to Kurt and tried to control the anger in her voice. "Have you forgotten how totally hateful she was to you? Have you forgotten how she laughed at you at the Hewitts' party? She's the one who named you Aquaman!"

"I asked her about that," Kurt said. "She

said it was just a joke. It is kind of funny, when you think about it."

"No, it isn't," Emma insisted. "It's her way of belittling you."

Kurt reached out and touched Emma's hand. "Maybe we both took that whole incident too seriously," he said softly. "I think she'd like to be your friend."

That was too much for Emma to handle. She jumped up again and stared at Kurt. "My friend? My *friend?*" She repeated incredulously. "Are you crazy? No one in my entire life has ever been meaner or more cruel to me than Diana De Bitch, and here you are defending her!"

"I'm only trying to be fair," Kurt said piously. "There's no reason for you to call her names. It's beneath you."

"Oh! How . . . how dare you?" Emma seethed. She was totally livid. "When you get that sanctimonious look on your face I just want to kill you!"

Kurt stood up and faced Emma. "Look, I'm sorry you hate her. But you can't tell me who my friends should be, Emma."

"How can you be so dense?" Emma cried.

"I think we should both just chill out before we say things we might regret," Kurt said.

"Right now, Kurt Ackerman, my biggest regret is ever getting involved with you!"

"You don't mean that—"

"I don't?" Emma exploded. "You're supposed to love me! You're supposed to be on my side!"

"This is not an adversarial situation, for Pete's sake!" Kurt yelled. "You are acting like a spoiled brat who can't get her own way!"

Emma had never been so angry in her life. If she'd been a guy she would have belted him. As it was, all she could do was turn on her heel, walk out of the room, and slam the door behind her as hard as her 110 pounds would allow.

SEVEN

Emma made her way through the bodies in the living room until she finally found Sam. She and Trent were simultaneously slow-dancing and sipping champagne. Emma interrupted them and dragged Sam into a relatively private corner of the massive kitchen.

"What is going on?" Sam asked with concern. Emma had a very weird look on her face.

"I'm leaving," Emma said. "Can you get a ride?"

"What do you mean, you're leaving?" Sam echoed. "What happened?"

Emma clenched her fists and bit her lip to keep from crying right there in the kitchen. "I just had another fight with Kurt," she said, trying to keep her voice low. "I have to get out of here."

"It'll probably blow over," Sam said. "Maybe you should just take a walk outside to cool off."

"I don't want to cool off. I want to kill him," Emma seethed.

Out of the corner of her eye Sam saw Diana cross the room. "Is it something about Diana?"

"It's everything about Diana," Emma answered. "Kurt thinks Diana is just swell," she spat out. "He was actually *defending* her to me, can you believe it?"

"Lame," Sam said, shaking her head. "But listen, if you break up with Kurt you'll play right into her hand. That's what she wants, and then she'll win. You've got to fight for him!"

"Oh, Sam, if he really loved me I wouldn't have to fight for him at all!" Emma could feel the tears welling up in her eyes. "I have to go," she whispered. She desperately wanted to leave before anyone saw her cry.

"Ha-ha-ha-ha!" Sam started laughing maniacally. Emma stared at her, thinking she had lost her mind. But when Sam twirled Emma around so she could see that Diana was coming their way, Sam's odd laughter suddenly made sense.

"That's the funniest story I ever heard in my life!" Sam said, still laughing raucously. She pretended to wipe tears of laughter from her eyes. "Oh, hi, Diana!" she chirped, feigning surprise. "Emma was just telling me the most hilarious story about you on the beach in a bikini, having some trouble with a tampon string. You really should have been more careful!"

"I don't know what you're talking about," Diana said, taken aback.

"Oh, well, I don't blame you," Sam commiserated. "If it happened to me I wouldn't want the story to get around, either. It must have been incredibly embarrassing!"

"You are full of it," Diana said, tossing her curls. She got a glass of water from the sink. "Having fun, Emma?" she asked cattily.

"Well, actually I'm a little bored," Emma said, trying hard to look it.

"Really? On a date with Aquaman? Funny, I find him anything but boring."

"Oh, Diana, don't give me that," Emma spat out. "You have no interest in Kurt. You're flirting with him just to bug me."

"My, my, aren't we egocentric?" Diana

chided. "Did it ever occur to you that I might really like him?"

"No. I know you better than that," Emma said. "What he's got is not the kind of thing you and your shallow buddies consider important."

"And what would that be?" Diana asked, a small condescending smile on her lips.

"Character. Integrity. Loyalty," Emma said loftily.

"Well, let me ask you a question, Emma dearest," Diana asked. "If Aquaman has so much character and integrity and loyalty, why is he always flirting with me?"

Before Emma could frame a retort, Diana had sashayed out of the kitchen.

"Diana is a life form that is low on the food chain," Sam observed.

Emma covered her eyes with her hands. "She's right," she whispered.

"About what?" Sam asked.

"About Kurt. If he was really all those things I said he was, he'd stand by me. And he wouldn't give someone like Diana the time of day."

"Oh, Em . . ." Sam felt so bad for her. She knew that Emma really loved Kurt. It was terrible for her to find out that he might not be quite as perfect as she had imagined.

"Ms. Bridges!" Trent said, sidling up next to Sam in the kitchen. "My champagne is losing its fizz. What do you say we grab a fresh bottle and go look at the stars?"

"I'm a little busy with Emma right now," Sam said.

"Oh, believe me, Emma's one girl who can take care of herself. Isn't that right, Emma?"

Emma managed a sad smile. "I always have, haven't I?"

"See?" Trent said, putting an arm around Sam's waist.

"Are you sure?" Sam asked Emma. "I'll leave with you if you want."

"She wouldn't think of it," Trent said, answering quickly for Emma.

Sam unwrapped Trent's arm from her waist and faced him. "Trent, I'm busy. Go pop a cork or something. I'll meet you by the pool."

Trent kissed Sam on the cheek. "I won't start without you," he promised, walking away.

"He's as droll as ever," Emma said wryly.

"He rented a yacht for tomorrow," Sam said eagerly. "He invited me."

"Believe me, Sam, Trent's appeal wanes real fast."

"Well, it'll last long enough to get me on my first yacht, that's for sure," Sam said with a shrug. "Anyway, I'm wise to him. He's so jaded by always getting whatever he wants that the cooler I act, the harder he'll pursue me."

"I thought you were crazy about Pres," Emma said.

"Pres is broke, Trent is rich," Sam pointed out philosophically.

"You know, Sam, money does not necessarily make you happy."

Sam smiled ironically. "Why is it that rich people are the only ones who ever say that?"

Emma had no answer for that. She pulled her car keys from her purse and looped the strap over her shoulder.

"Have fun," Emma said in a sad voice.

"Do you mind?" Sam asked quickly. "I mean about me and Trent? I know you two used to—"

"No, we never really used to anything, not from my point of view, anyway." Emma nervously pushed her hair behind one ear. "You think Kurt knows I'm still here? I don't want to run into him on my way out."

"I'll scope it out for you," Sam offered.

Emma leaned against the counter and fiddled with the car keys while Sam staked out Kurt's whereabouts. Suddenly she felt completely exhausted. She wanted so badly for someone to comfort her, to make everything okay. But who could she turn to? Obviously not Kurt. And Sam was all wound up in pursuing the life-style of the rich and famous. Emma had always felt that she could confide in Carrie, but she was so crazy about Billy that she seemed to be in an altered state of consciousness lately—there, but not really there. Well, Emma knew that state well. She'd recently been there with Kurt. Now she wondered if she'd ever be there again.

"Emma! Still here?" It was Trent, carrying his open bottle of champagne by the neck. He took a swig. "Ah, great stuff." He held the bottle out to Emma, who shook her head. "I came back inside to find a towel for Daffy Daphne. She seems to have misplaced her clothing. It is not a pretty sight."

Emma tried to smile and failed.

"You okay?" Trent asked with concern.

He sounded as if he really cared, and that got to Emma. After all, she'd known him forever, and she really did need a shoulder to cry on.

"Would you give me a hug?" she asked in a small voice.

Without a word Trent put his arms around her. So what if it was only Trent? It felt so good just to be held.

"Want to talk about it?" Trent asked.

Before Emma could answer, Sam loped back into the kitchen. "The coast is clear. I couldn't find him anywhere," she said.

Trent's arms dropped away from Emma as soon as he saw Sam. "You look thirsty," he said, lifting the bottle of champagne in Sam's direction.

She accepted the bottle and took a swig. "There's something very decadent about swilling good champagne from the bottle," she said. "I could get used to it."

Trent took a step toward Sam. "Swill away," he said, sliding his hand around her slender waist.

Emma looked from Trent to Sam. They both looked quite self-satisfied, and quite smitten with each other. So much for Trent being devastated by her falling for another guy. Wasn't anyone in the world ever sincere about anything?

She said good-bye and walked down the driveway, but before she got into the car, she looked up at the starry sky. She remembered her very first date with Kurt, when he had taken her around to see the parts of his island the tourists didn't know. They had walked on the beach, and she had wished on a shooting star that he would kiss her, and then he had. A silent tear rolled down Emma's cheek. Now she knew that even if wishes did come true, they didn't necessarily stay that way. Dejectedly she climbed into the car and drove home.

When she got up to her room she pulled off her clothes and let them fall on the floor, something she never did. She put on a T-shirt and climbed into bed, then pulled her journal out of the drawer in her nightstand. Emma's aunt Liz had given her the journal just before she'd left for Sunset Island. It meant a lot to her. Liz was her favorite relative—the only one she was close to, actually—and writing in her journal had provided solace through many a bad moment.

When she opened the small tapestry-covered book she realized she hadn't written in it in days. When everything was going well she didn't feel compelled to record her thoughts.

It seems impossible, but I think Kurt and I are really finished. My heart is breaking. He said he loved me—that's the line I keep hearing over and over in my head. But if you really love someone, it has to be more than words. As Sam says, talk is cheap. I thought Kurt was the most wonderful, most perfect guy in the world. But maybe he's not to blame. Maybe it's me. Maybe I'm just not worth loving.

Emma bit the end of her pen and stared at what she had written. Would she end up like her mother, caring only about superficial things, having this lifted or that tucked in an effort to make herself lovable?

"No!" Emma said fiercely. "That's not what I'm going to be!" She clicked her pen and began writing again.

I remember Daddy coming home once when I was little, and he had the saddest look on his face. Something terrible had gone wrong in his business, and

*he'd lost a lot of money. I heard him tell
Mother that it was all his fault, and I
expected her to put her arms around
him and comfort him, because that's
what I wanted to do. But she didn't. She
just nodded her head and agreed that
the trouble really was all his fault. And
then she left to go to an art exhibit.*

Tears blurred Emma's vision as she
wrote. It was a sad memory, one she hadn't
even realized she had. She laid her head on
her pillow and let the tears come. It felt
good finally to let go. Maybe Kurt wouldn't
turn out to be the great love of her life, and
that possibility hurt, because Emma knew
that if Kurt came to her sad and defeated,
she would stick by him and put her arms
around him, no matter what. The question
was, would he do the same for her?

EIGHT

Saturday morning Emma awoke to the sound of rain pelting her window. There was an occasional grumble of thunder, and the dark sky lit up with streaks of lightning. Great, just great. Here it was her day off and the monsoons had arrived. At least the weather matched her mood.

She rolled over, hoping to fall back asleep. Maybe if she tried hard enough she could sleep right through until tomorrow. A rainy day off left her entirely too much time to think, and thinking was just too painful.

Emma actually did doze off for a while, but she was awakened by a light tap on her door.

"Come in," she called groggily from her bed.

In walked Katie, dressed in her favorite

pink bathing suit, clutching her inflatable duck in one hand and her doll, Sally, in the other. The family mutt, appropriately named Dog, followed Katie into the room, trying to grab Sally out of her hand.

"I'm ready for the beach," Katie chirped.

Oh, no! Kurt had promised to take Katie to the beach today!

"Honey, it's raining," Emma said. "We can't go to the beach in the rain."

"Yes, we can," Katie insisted.

Emma patted the bed next to her, and Katie climbed up next to her. "People don't go to the beach in the rain because they'd get all wet," Emma explained.

"But I thought the reason we swimmed was to get all wet," Katie said, her face scrunched up in confusion.

"Yes, that's true," Emma said. This was proving more difficult to explain that she had anticipated. "But the beach isn't safe during a storm. Sometimes there's lightning and thunder, so it's best to stay inside."

"Lightning and thunder can't come inside?" Katie asked, wide-eyed.

"No, honey, they can't."

Katie considered this. Emma knew she really didn't like thunder and lightning, but she really didn't want to miss her day at the beach, either.

"Can me and Kurt play inside, then?" Katie asked hopefully.

"Uh, where's your mom?" Emma asked, changing the subject. Maybe Jane had planned something to do with Katie, since it was raining out.

"She left," Katie pouted. "And Daddy is playing trains with Wills and Dougie. There's nothing for me to do."

At that moment Jeff Hewitt appeared at Emma's door. "There's the midget," Jeff said, crossing to Emma's bed and scooping Katie into his arms. "Sorry, Emma, I know it's your day off."

"Oh, it's okay," Emma assured him. "I was just explaining that we couldn't go to the beach in the rain."

"You and Wills are too busy, Daddy," Katie pouted.

"Come help us put the train together to surprise Ethan when he gets home from his camping trip, okay?"

"Can we get ice cream first?" Katie asked.

"It's not even lunchtime yet," Jeff said with a laugh.

"After lunch?" Katie prodded.

"Yes, after lunch." Jeff smiled at Emma. "She's just like her mother—a very tough negotiator." He planted a huge noisy kiss on his daughter's cheek.

"Daddy!" Katie squealed happily as he carried her from the room.

Emma pulled the covers over her head. Other people's happiness made her feel gloomier than ever. She heard the phone ring, and then Jeff yelled upstairs that it was for her.

"Hello?"

"Hi, it's Carrie."

"Oh, hi," Emma said listlessly.

"You're mad at me about last night, aren't you?" Carrie said quickly. "I'm sorry. I acted like the kind of girls I can't stand, the ones who get so preoccupied with a guy that they ditz out on their friends—"

"Hey, I'm not mad at you!" Emma interrupted.

"Really?" Carrie asked. "You can tell me if you are."

"Really," Emma assured her.

"Well, that's a relief," Carrie said. "So did you have fun? We left shortly after I saw you."

"Oh, Carrie, it was horrible!" Emma cried. "My life is ruined."

"God, what happened?"

"I had another fight with Kurt. A really devastating one. Diana is going after him, and she's succeeding."

"I just can't believe that," Carrie said.

"Believe it. They were in each other's arms when I showed up at the party. And he defended her to me over and over. He knows how awful she's been to me my whole life. If he really loved me, how could he do that?"

"I just can't believe Kurt could be such a hypocrite!" Carrie said. "I mean, he's always had such contempt for rich kids who flaunt their money, which is the very definition of Diana De Witt. It just doesn't make any sense!"

"Unless he's not quite as noble as he professes to be," Emma said sadly.

"You mean you think that if Diana was poor he wouldn't give her the time of day?" Carrie asked.

"I don't know what to think anymore."

"I'm so sorry, Emma. Is there anything I can do?"

"Got a gun?" Emma asked morosely.

"I think there's a law against killing your boyfriend without a permit," Carrie pointed out.

"Okay, I'll just maim him, then," Emma said. "But I'll kill Diana. I'll say I did it for the good of society. They'll probably name a street after me."

"I have an idea. Today's your day off, right?" Carrie asked.

"Right. I'm spending it with my head under the covers."

"Well, maybe I could talk you out of that. How about if I take you to lunch at the Play Café, my treat? You can cry on my shoulder or scream or we can not talk about it at all—whatever you want."

"I'd be terrible company," Emma said softly.

"I like terrible company," Carrie assured her. "Come on. I know you'll return the favor if I ever need it."

Emma smiled into the phone. Carrie was such a great person. "Okay, you talked me into it."

"Great!" Carrie said. "I'll meet you there in, say, an hour?"

"Fine," Emma said. "I'll enjoy walking through the storm. The weather matches my mood."

"And I'll enjoy driving Claudia's Porsche." Carrie laughed. "Okay, see you soon."

"Carrie?"

"What?"

"Thanks," Emma said softly before she hung up.

Emma donned her raincoat but went out into the foul weather bareheaded. It felt good to walk against the wind and to feel the rain pelting her face. There was hardly anyone out, either in cars or on foot. It made the island seem like an entirely different place. For once the café was almost empty. Emma was glad. She definitely did not want to run into any of the regulars. She found Carrie already at their usual table. She had taken off a big red plastic poncho and a sweatshirt and was draping them over a chair.

"Oh, hi! I just got here." Carrie said, happy to see Emma. She pushed a lock of wet hair out of her eyes. "This rain will make my hair frizz, for sure." She gave a philosophical shrug. "Ah, well, such is life." She picked up two menus and handed one to Emma.

"I know this by heart," Emma protested.

"No, you don't. It's just that you always order one of two things—a salad or a hamburger. I say let's chart new culinary territory." Carrie scanned the menu. "Aha! See this? Did you know they had fried oysters?"

"No," Emma admitted.

"Well, I for one have never eaten an oyster. In fact, I'm not even sure what an oyster is. I intend to try them," she announced bravely. "Your turn."

Emma had not only eaten oysters but had eaten them raw—in Cannes, on the coast of France—just the previous summer. Of course, she was not about to tell Carrie that for fear of sounding like someone she hated, someone like Diana De Witt, maybe.

"I'll have them, too," Emma said.

"There, now, don't you feel better already?" Carrie asked. "Food defiance is the first step toward a real 'who cares' attitude."

Emma smiled. Carrie was trying hard to cheer her up.

"Really, how are you doing?" Carrie asked quietly.

Emma shrugged. "The same, I guess."

"I was thinking of what you said about Kurt on my way over here," Carrie said. "The only thing I can figure is that maybe you didn't know him as well as you thought you did."

"Maybe," Emma agreed sadly.

Carrie nodded. "To tell you the truth, that scares me, because I'm crazy about Billy and I feel as if I know him so well. But that's exactly how you felt about Kurt."

Emma nodded in agreement.

"So how do you ever know, really? How can you be sure?"

"I certainly don't have any answers for you," Emma said. "If I did I wouldn't feel so miserable."

"You're right," Carrie said. "I'm sorry. I just turned the whole conversation around so that it was about me. I can't stand people who do that!"

"It's okay, Carrie."

"No, is isn't. It's obnoxious. I'm an intelligent person! I have to have more on my mind than one stupid guy!"

The waitress brought their fried oysters and Carrie dug into hers with gusto.

"Mmm, I like them!" she said. "I still don't know what they are, but I like them."

Emma took a small bite of an oyster. It would barely go down her throat. She put her fork down and sipped at her iced tea.

"You're too upset to eat," Carrie noticed.

"Oh, Carrie, I just about want to die!" Emma whispered passionately.

The front door of the café banged open, and Daphne ran inside. She was wearing a tiny pair of shorts and a T-shirt that the rain had plastered to her body. She was a shocking sight. Every one of her bones was clearly visible through the wet, clinging material. Her legs had gone from skinny to emaciated, and she reminded Emma of photos she'd seen of people in concentration camps. Emma shivered. This girl obviously belonged in a hospital.

Daphne stood just inside the door, her teeth chattering and her whole body shivering violently. Carrie and Emma looked at each other for a moment. Then Carrie grabbed her sweatshirt from the chair and went to Daphne.

"Here, put his on," Carrie instructed Daphne.

Daphne looked dazed, as if she couldn't quite focus on what she was hearing. Carrie slipped the girl's arms into the sweatshirt as if she were a small child, then zipped it up, led her to their table, and helped her sit down.

"I guess you got caught in the rain," Emma said. It occurred to her that this was the first time she'd ever seen Daphne without Lorell or Diana. It seemed hard to believe that Daphne could actually function on her own. Well, judging by the way she was acting, maybe she couldn't.

"I went shopping," Daphne said, "at the Cheap Boutique."

Emma and Carrie nodded. The boutique was right across the street from the café.

"There's something wrong with the mirrors in there," Daphne croaked, her eyes narrowing. "Somebody did something to them. They made me look fat, like those trick mirrors at the circus." She tried to smile, but the result was a weird grimace that never reached her eyes. "So I just ran out of the store. Nothing in there would fit a pig like me."

"Daphne—" Emma began.

"Who would play a trick like that?" Daphne asked. Her eyes looked really crazy. She glanced from Emma to Carrie and back to Emma, shivering so hard that her body vibrated.

"Daphne, I think maybe you're sick," Carrie said gently. "Can we take you somewhere?"

"Where?" Daphne looked puzzled.

"The emergency room at the clinic, maybe?" Carrie suggested.

Daphne stood up so violently that she knocked her chair over. The noise brought the waitress from the kitchen. She stood behind the counter, trying to decide what to do.

"Do you think I'm crazy?" Daphne screamed.

"No," Emma protested, "we just think you need some help—"

"You did it!" Daphne shouted at Emma. "You changed the mirrors because you're jealous of me."

"Daphne, really—" Emma began, reaching out for her arm.

"I hate you!" Daphne screamed. She picked up Emma's iced tea glass and cracked it against the edge of the table. Shards of glass flew everywhere as the tumbler shattered. Wielding the jagged bottom of the glass, Daphne lunged at Emma, who jumped out of her way. The waitress screamed.

"Daphne, give me the glass," Carrie said in a steady voice, holding out her hand.

But Daphne had her eyes glued to Emma. "I'm going to kill you for changing those mirrors."

Everything happened in a blur. Someone

111

opened the front door just as Daphne leapt at Emma, still jabbing the air with the broken glass. Carrie reached for the glass, but Daphne dodged her and again darted toward Emma, backing her into a corner and striking out with the jagged weapon.

Instinctively Emma lifted her right arm to protect her face, but she felt the quick bite of razor-sharp glass slicing into her wrist. Strong hands seized Daphne from behind, pulling her elbows back until she was forced to drop the glass.

Daphne let out an eerie, unreal scream.

Only then did Emma notice dimly that her arm was bleeding and that the strong arms that had kept Daphne from slicing her face open belonged to Kurt Ackerman.

NINE

"You're really very lucky," the young doctor told Emma as he put the final stitches in her right wrist. "That cut just missed an artery."

As he bandaged her wrist and wrapped it in layer after layer of gauze, Emma closed her eyes and tried to think straight. Everything had happened so quickly. The police, summoned by the waitress, had arrived almost immediately after Emma was injured. When Daphne saw the police she got hysterical. At first she stared at the shattered glass in her hand as if someone else were wielding it. Then she fell to her knees, and screamed maniacally until the police managed to get her under control. They saw that Emma obviously needed help, too—her wrist was dripping blood. Kurt had volunteered to drive her to the clinic so that she would not have to ride in the squad car with Daphne.

Emma shook off the horrible memory as the doctor finished wrapping her wrist. "You okay?" he asked her, noticing how pale she looked. "You can lie down for a while, if you like."

"No, I'm all right." Emma managed to get down from the examining table.

"Just stop at the front desk on your way out," the doctor said.

Emma walked unsteadily to the reception area, where Carrie, Kurt, and a police officer sat waiting for her.

"You okay?" Carrie asked, rushing to Emma.

She nodded weakly and sat down. She couldn't meet Kurt's eyes.

"I'm Officer Casey," the tall red-haired policeman said politely. "Do you feel up to making a report on this?"

Emma nodded. She went over exactly what had happened. "And then Kurt grabbed Daphne, and then you showed up," Emma concluded.

Officer Casey wrote everything down and verified the spelling of everyone's name.

"Do you want to file criminal assault charges?" he asked Emma.

"No!" Emma said quickly. "Daphne's sick! She needs help!"

"That doesn't necessarily make her any less responsible for attacking you, Miss Cresswell," the officer pointed out. "If you change your mind, you can call me at the station house."

"Where is Daphne now?" Emma asked.

"She's here. The doctor sedated her," Officer Casey said. "I believe they're trying to reach her parents to get permission to transfer her to Memorial Hospital in Bangor."

"Her parents are in Europe," Kurt volunteered. Everyone looked at him. "I'm, um, a friend of her houseguest, and she told me," he added lamely.

"Well, according to her driver's license she's of age," the officer said, "but she's in no condition to make any decisions now." He made a note on his police report. "Excuse me a minute. I have to call in." He zipped into his rain gear and walked out to the squad car.

At that moment an attractive young woman came over to the group. "I'm Dr. Simms," she said. "Daphne is very ill. We've reached a Thomas Whittinger, her older brother. He'll be here shortly. We couldn't locate the parents."

"Will she be okay?" Carrie asked.

"She's a very sick girl," Dr. Simms said. "She's obviously suffering from late-stage anorexia nervosa, and she also appears to be on some kind of drug, probably amphetamines—speed—to help her lose weight."

"Will she be okay?" Emma asked.

"That is a question I cannot answer," the doctor said brusquely. "Are you friends of hers?"

"Sort of," Kurt murmured.

"Well, anyone with eyes can see that this girl is gravely ill, so let me ask you this: did any of you do anything about it?"

"We aren't her friends, really," Carrie explained. "She hangs out with an entirely different group. I mean, she just attacked Emma!"

The doctor looked them over and nodded. She seemed to want to say more, but she didn't. She just excused herself and walked away.

"I feel awful," Emma whispered.

"Should I get the doctor?" Carrie asked quickly.

"No, I mean about Daphne. How many times have I told myself that she was sick? I just never did anything about it."

"Oh, come on," Carrie said. "There was nothing we could do. Maybe her so-called friends could have, or her houseguest," Carrie added, looking meaningfully at Kurt, "but Daphne wouldn't have taken any kind of advice from us."

"I don't know," Emma said. "I still feel as if I should have tried to do something instead of just saying it wasn't my problem."

There was an awkward silence, during which Emma and Kurt looked everywhere except at each other.

"Excuse me," Carrie said, obviously wanting to leave them alone for a while. "I'm going to make a phone call."

"Are you okay?" Kurt finally asked, when Carrie was out of earshot.

Emma nodded. "Thank you for . . . you know," she said. "How did you happen to walk into the café just then?"

"I was looking for you," Kurt said. "I called the Hewitts, and Jeff said you'd gone out to lunch with Carrie. I guessed you'd go to the café."

"Well, I'm glad you guessed right," Emma said softly.

"Me, too," Kurt said.

Silence. Emma cleared her throat. "So why were you looking for me?"

Kurt sighed and ran his hand through his hair nervously. "It, um, doesn't seem very appropriate to ask you now."

"Oh, everything's so mixed up, I don't see how it could matter," Emma said.

"Well, the thing is, Lorell is using her dad's pilot and jet to fly to New York tomorrow for the Conquest concert at Madison Square Garden. She and Diana have invited a bunch of kids to go with them, and I thought you might like to come," Kurt said.

Emma stared at him. "Surely Lorell and Diana won't go now that Daphne is so sick," she said. "I mean, Diana is Daphne's houseguest!"

"I really don't know," Kurt said. "Maybe she'll just visit Daphne when she gets back."

"Who invited you on this trip, anyway?" Emma asked, "Lorell or Diana?"

"What difference does it make?" Kurt said. "It's not dates. It's just a bunch of friends."

"Those people are not my friends," Emma said, "and I can't believe you really think they're yours."

Kurt's face hardened. "I don't want to fight with you, Emma. I came to ask you to see if you could get a day off and come with me because I want you to be there."

"How can *you* get a day off?" Emma asked. "And how can you possibly afford this trip?"

"That's not really your problem, is it?"

"No, I guess not," Emma said sadly. "Not anymore."

"That means you won't come?" Kurt asked.

"Kurt, those people want me along even less than I want to go with them."

"Diana asked me to invite you!" Kurt protested.

"Right." Emma laughed sardonically. "Because she was absolutely certain that I would say no, and she would look like this wonderful human being for having invited me."

Kurt looked down at his clenched hands. "I . . . I just don't know what to say to you anymore, Emma."

Emma gulped hard. "There's nothing to say, I guess."

A tall heavyset young man with thin, dripping wet blond hair came running into the clinic, his open raincoat flapping behind him. He hurried over to Kurt. "How's my sister?" he asked.

"You better ask the doctor," Kurt said. "This is Thomas, Daphne's brother," he told Emma.

Thomas nodded. "Excuse me." He hurried over to the admissions desk.

"Just out of curiosity, how do you happen to know Daphne's brother?" Emma asked Kurt.

"I met him at the Whittingers'," Kurt said uncomfortably.

"Yes, I figured that out," Emma said. "I'm also bright enough to know you weren't over there visiting Daphne at the time, either."

"Em, they have a tennis court. Diana invited me over to play, that's all."

"I'll *bet* she invited you over to play," Emma retorted. She felt tired. The pain-killer the doctor had given her was making everything seem surreal. How could all this be happening? she wondered. One day her life had been great, and the next day every-thing was crazy, frightening, out of control.

"You don't look so good," Kurt said with concern in his voice.

"I . . . I just feel . . . Oh, Kurt, I'm so sad," Emma said, gulping back tears. "Maybe it's just a delayed reaction to being attacked by Daphne, or maybe it's the medication." She leaned her head back against the wall. Kurt gently pulled her toward him until she was cradled in his arms.

"I'm very tired," she whispered, tears running down her face.

Officer Casey came back into the waiting room, conferred with the admitting nurse, then walked over to Emma and Kurt. "Thomas Whittinger has signed papers for his sister to be transferred to Memorial Hospital." He handed Emma a slip of paper. "This is the number you should call if you change your mind about pressing criminal charges, Miss Cresswell."

"Thank you," Emma said, taking the paper, "but I won't change my mind."

The officer left just as Carrie returned from the bank of pay phones. "What's happened?" she asked.

"Daphne's brother came, and they're transferring her to Memorial. That's all we know," Kurt said, his arm still around Emma.

"How are you feeling?" Carrie asked Emma.

"Like I've been run over by a truck," Emma said.

"It's probably the codeine in that pain-killer," Carrie said.

"Come on." Kurt helped Emma up. "I'll drive you home."

Emma signed a form at the billing desk while Kurt talked to Thomas Whittinger, and then all three went out to Kurt's car. The storm had finally let up. Kurt concentrated on skirting the flooded areas of the road as he drove carefully to the Hewitts' house. No one seemed to be in the mood for conversation.

"Want me to come in with you?" Carrie asked when they arrived.

"If you wouldn't mind," Emma said gratefully. She wasn't up to explaining to everyone what had happened. She just wanted to sleep for a long, long time.

"I'll call you," Kurt told Emma as he helped her gingerly from the car.

"Are you going on the trip tomorrow with Diana?" Emma asked him.

"I told you, I'm not going with Diana," Kurt said. "I'm just going."

"I see," Emma said quietly.

"Look, I know you're very blasé about

122

New York City," Kurt said. "You've been there hundreds of times. But I've never been there. Besides, I invited you to come."

Emma stared at him sadly. He looked so earnest, but they might as well have been speaking two different languages.

"If you're going on that trip tomorrow, don't bother to call me," Emma finally said.

Carrie carefully walked a few steps away from them and pretended to be fascinated at the sight of Dog running around the front yard.

"Emma, you don't mean that," Kurt said.

"Yes, I do."

"I can't believe you'd break up with me because I'm going to New York!" he said incredulously.

"Who's paying for your trip, Kurt?" Emma asked.

"I told you, that's not really your—"

"Diana's paying, right?" Emma interrupted. "Do you think I'm too stupid to figure that out?"

"So what if she is?" Kurt shot back. "At least she's honest about having money. She isn't trying to pretend she's something she's not."

"Meaning you think I am," Emma said in a low voice.

"Meaning that you confuse me, Emma," Kurt said. He sighed and stared off into the distance. "Look, this isn't the time to have this conversation. They've got you all drugged up, and you've just been through hell. Let's talk after you get some rest," he suggested.

"No, Kurt. I can't keep going through this," Emma said wearily. She turned toward the house, her vision blurring with tears.

"Emma—" Kurt called after her.

But there was nothing left to say, so even though her heart was breaking, she didn't turn around.

TEN

When Emma woke up, rain was pelting her window once again. Her wrist was throbbing, and she was in a fog. She had absolutely no idea how long she'd slept.

Carrie had helped her explain everything that had happened to an astonished Jane and Jeff Hewitt. They had been sympathetic and sincerely concerned for Emma's well-being. Then Carrie had come upstairs and stayed until Emma crawled into bed, and that was the last thing she remembered.

She turned to look at her clock. Six o'clock. She'd been asleep for almost four hours. Next to the clock she saw a small prescription bottle and a note: "Emma, I got your prescription filled for you. Call me when you wake up. Carrie. P.S. Call Sam, too. She's worried."

Emma padded into the bathroom and swallowed a pain pill, then crawled back into bed. There was absolutely no good reason to get up. As the medication took effect, she drifted asleep again and dreamed a monster with chestnut curls was holding her head underwater. Dimly she heard someone at her door and groggily opened her eyes.

"Emma? Are you okay?" Jane said. "I thought I heard you cry out"

"I'm okay," Emma said. "I had a terrible dream."

Jane walked over and sat on the edge of Emma's bed. "How are you feeling?"

"Weird," Emma said.

"It's the codeine in those pills, probably," Jane said. "When you stop taking those painkillers in a day or two that feeling will go away."

"I'm really sorry, Jane. I'm creating a lot of trouble for you."

"Please!" Jane said. "It's hardly your fault that Daphne attacked you. I just wish I'd said something to her parents. I could see she was sick."

"That's how I feel, too," Emma said.

Jane sighed. "Her parents are rarely on the island. And frankly, I can't stand them. It's all just very, very sad."

The two sat companionably for a minute, listening to the rain slanting against Emma's window.

"Carrie called this afternoon while you were sleeping," Jane said. "When you feel up to it you might want to call her back. She's really concerned about you."

"I will," Emma promised.

"Well, just holler if you need anything," Jane said, getting up. "And take tomorrow off if you don't feel like working."

"Thanks, Jane, for . . . well, for everything," Emma said quietly.

"*De nada.*" Emma caught Jane's understanding smile before she closed the bedroom door behind her.

Emma switched on the small lamp on her nightstand and dialed Carrie's number.

"Hello?"

Emma recognized the voice of the Templetons' four-year-old daughter. "Hi, Chloe, it's Emma. Is Carrie there?"

"Uh-uh," said Chloe. "I'm playing Barbies," she added. "Mommy!" she screamed.

"Hello?" came Claudia's Templeton's voice.

"Hi, this is Emma Cresswell. I was trying to reach Carrie."

"She went to Bangor with Flirting with

Danger," Claudia said. "Billy wrote a song for her, and he's singing it tonight."

"That's right, she told me. I forgot," Emma said.

"She told me what happened to you today," Claudia said. "It must have been awful. How are you feeling?"

"I'm okay," Emma said. She felt embarrassed to realize that the whole island would be talking about what had happened. She had inherited a loathing for what her mother called "creating a scene."

"Do you want me to leave her a note?" Claudia asked. "I'm sure she'll be home late."

"Please just tell her I called and I'm okay," Emma said, "if you wouldn't mind."

"No problem," Claudia assured her.

Emma hung up and dialed Sam's number.

"Jacobs's Morgue, you kill 'em, we chill 'em," came the voice of one of the twins.

"Hi, it's Emma. Is Sam there?"

"Whoa, Emma! Sam told us what happened," the twin said. "Were you, like, freaked to death?"

"I'm fine," Emma said tersely, hoping to cut off further conversation. Even the twins already knew what had happened. That

128

meant the story would probably be a head-line in the *Breakers* tomorrow.

"I'll get Sam," the twin volunteered. "Hey, just think. Now whenever people see the scar on your wrist they'll think you tried to off yourself. It'll be very dramatic!" the girl said cheerfully.

"Hi," Sam said, finally getting the phone. "How are you?"

"I'm okay," Emma said.

"Carrie called me from the clinic this after-noon," Sam said. "I wanted to come right over, but I was alone here with the monsters. I didn't dare bring them because they're read-ing Edgar Allan Poe, and they're obsessed with morbidity at the moment."

"I was, too, when I read Poe's stories," Emma said.

"Did you practice making yourself up with a deathlike pallor and write out instructions for your burial outfit in case you met an untimely death?"

"Maybe those girls should be in therapy," Emma suggested.

"Mr. Jacobs says it's a stage. He calls all their weird stuff 'a stage.' Anyway, the twins are going to the movies with their dad and Stephanie," she said, naming Mr. Jacobs's girlfriend. "Want me to come over? Or do you feel like being alone?"

"I'd love it if you'd come," Emma said truthfully. "I might be awful company, though. I'm taking this pain medication that makes everthing seem sort of foggy."

"Oh, must have codeine in it," Sam said. "I took that when I broke my arm, my ankle, and my collarbone."

"All at once?" Emma asked, horrified.

"No. Three different accidents. I went through a klutzy stage when I was in junior high. The only good part was the drugs," Sam said philosophically. "I hated junior high so much that being in a fog was a relief. I'll be there in a few," she promised.

Sam bopped in a half hour later with a pint of rum raisin ice cream and two spoons. "I come bearing gifts," she said, plopping the ice cream on the bed and herself into a chair. She looked at Emma's bandaged wrist. "Does it hurt?"

Emma shook her head as Sam took the lid off the ice cream and dug in. "Mmm, rum raisin will cure anything," Sam said blissfully, holding the ice cream out to Emma.

"Just the thought makes me queasy," Emma said.

Sam shrugged and spooned more ice cream into her mouth. "Carrie told me about Kurt showing up and holding Daphne until the cops came," Sam said. "Good thing, huh?"

"Good thing," Emma echoed sadly. Breaking up with Kurt hurt much more than her wrist ever could.

"So are you guys back together?" Sam asked hopefully.

"It's over," Emma said. "I mean completely over."

"But I thought he took you to the clinic and everything. . . ."

"He did."

"So then, why?" Sam looked confused.

"It's just . . . everything," Emma said sadly. "You know why he came to look for me this afternoon? He wanted to invite me to go with Lorell and Diana and Lord knows who else on Lorell's daddy's jet to Manhattan tomorrow for the Conquest concert."

"Kurt's going?" Sam looked decidedly uncomfortable.

"Yes! Can you believe it?" Emma cried. "He says Diana told him to invite me. Sure! As if she wasn't certain I'd say no. And listen to this: Diana's paying for Kurt—and he's letting her!"

"Well, that doesn't seem so awful," Sam said carefully.

"Are you kidding? Kurt has more disdain for the idle rich than anyone I've ever known! Or so he said." Emma added bitterly. "Maybe he's really just envious of them."

"Are you included in that idle–rich category?" Sam asked.

"I work, remember?" Emma said, clearly hurt by Sam's question.

"I just meant that no matter what you do, it's still your choice. You don't *have* to work."

"Should I apologize for that?" Emma asked.

Sam stood up and looked out the window for a second.

"The thing is, if I were rich I'd want to have fun with my money," Sam said softly. "I think it's great that Diana's generous enough to pay for her friends, since she can afford to."

Emma sat up straighter in bed and stared at Sam. "Wait a minute. Are you defending Diana De Witt to me?" she asked incredulously.

"I'm not defending her; I know what a

bitch she is," Sam said. "I'm just saying that her being generous isn't necessarily a bad thing."

"I can't believe what I'm hearing!" Emma cried. "I really can't!"

Sam walked back over to the chair. "It's not like I'm . . . taking sides against you or something!" Sam said earnestly.

"Well, that's how it feels!" Emma retorted. "You mean you think it's just fine for Kurt to go on this little jaunt?"

"I'm going, too." Sam's mumbled remark was barely audible. She studied her fingernails as if the red polish had suddenly become fascinating.

"You're what?" Emma asked.

Sam finally looked at her. "I'm going, too. Trent invited me when we were out on the yacht today."

"How could you do that?" Emma whispered.

Sam threw the empty ice cream container into the wastebasket across the room, making a perfect shot. "Why shouldn't I?" Sam asked.

"Why *shouldn't* you?" Emma repeated. "Why shouldn't you go with Lorell Courtland and Diana De Witt to New York? Do I really have to answer that question?"

"I told you, Trent is the one who invited me."

"So that makes it okay?" Emma exploded.

"God, Emma, don't act as if I'm betraying you," Sam said. "It isn't like that."

"Oh, isn't it?" Emma said frostily. "Well, then, you'll have to explain to me just exactly what it is."

"I hate it when you put on that snotty voice!" Sam cried. She took a deep breath and forced herself to calm down. "Look, Emma, it's not a big deal unless you make it into one."

"You're only going with Trent because he can afford it," Emma said bitterly.

"It's easy for you to judge me, isn't it?" Sam said. "You've never known what it's like to not be able to afford to do things like this." Sam pushed her curls out of her eyes and fiddled with a button on her denim shirt. "This isn't about me, anyway," Sam said evenly. "It's about you and Kurt. Kurt loves you, you know."

"Right," Emma said, almost choking on the word.

"He does," Sam affirmed. "Maybe he's not as perfect as you dreamed. Maybe he's playing Diana's little game because he's been a poor kid all his life, I don't know."

Emma stared at her. "I see you hypocrites stick together."

Sam blanched.

Oh, so the words hurt. Well, that was too bad, Emma thought. Sam had hurt Emma, too.

Sam picked up her purse from the floor. "So maybe we less-than-perfect mortals do stick together. Maybe we can't live up to your lofty expectations of us." She headed for the door.

"Is that your noble exit line?" Emma called to her bitterly. "Because it's all bull. You and Kurt—you're just inventing excuses for doing what you want to do. But that doesn't make it right!"

But Emma was talking to the air. Sam was gone.

ELEVEN

Jane and Jeff were clearly surprised when Emma came down to breakfast the next morning. They both looked up from the paper and stared at her. Wills, Katie, and Dougie all stopped chewing their cereal. It occurred to Emma dimly that Dougie had come over to the Hewitts' awfully early.

She had forced herself to get on her feet, certain that if she lay in bed and did nothing but think she'd go crazy. Then she had showered—awkwardly holding her injured arm outside the curtain—and managed to dress.

"What can I get you?" Jeff said, standing up from the table.

"I'm okay." Emma reached into the cupboard for a cup. Everything seemed a little awkward because she was right-handed and it was her right wrist that was injured. She set the kettle on the stove to boil. Jane and Jeff always drank coffee in the morning, but Emma still preferred tea.

"Are you sure you don't want to take the day off?" Jane asked.

"No, really, I'm fine," Emma said. "I took two over-the-counter painkillers instead of the codeine pills so that I'd be able to think."

Wills stared at her hugely bandaged wrist. "Did you really get stitches?" he asked, wide-eyed.

"I really did," Emma said, finding a tea bag.

"I had stitches once," Dougie said proudly. "I karate-chopped through the sliding glass doors in our family room."

"Awesome," Wills said, beaming at Dougie. Everything that Dougie did was awesome as far as Wills was concerned.

"So how come you needed stitches?" Dougie asked between bites of cereal.

"I . . . cut my wrist," Emma said. She had no idea how much Jeff and Jane had told the kids.

"Yeah, but like, how?" Dougie pressed.

"Mom said a girl cut you with a glass by mistake," Wills contributed. "Is that right?"

"Yes, that's right," Emma said. The kettle boiled and she awkwardly poured the water with her left hand.

"She's a mean girl!" Katie said with conviction.

"No, she . . . made a mistake, honey," Emma said.

"Right," Jane agreed, nodding at her daughter. "It was an accident."

"Boy, big mistake," Dougie said. "Is she blind or something?"

"Yeah," Wills echoed, taking his cue from Dougie. "What is she, blind?"

"She is not blind, and it's none of your business," Jeff said sternly. "Finish your breakfast."

The boys scowled and pushed their spoons around in the soggy cereal.

Jane just shook her head at them and then turned to Emma. "At least let me get you some juice and some toast," she said, as Emma joined them at the large breakfast table with her tea.

"Thanks," Emma said with a grateful smile at Jane. "Ethan's due home today, isn't he?" she added, sipping her tea.

"Yeah," Wills said. "Dougie slept over last night, and we finished putting the train set together to surprise Ethan. Dad helped," he added.

"You guys did most of it," Jeff said.

"I helped, too," Katie piped up.

"You did not," Wills said with disgust.

"Did, too! Did, too!" Katie screamed.

"Hey, guys, it's much too early for this," Jeff reprimanded them. "Wills, if you and Dougie are done with breakfast, please take the garbage out."

"Well, Katie didn't help," Wills said under his breath as he pushed back his chair and noisily went out with the garbage. Dougie followed him.

Jane put orange juice and toast down in front of Emma, then sat down next to her. "You know, I appreciate your offer to work today, but there's really not much for you to do," Jane said with a kind smile. "The whole family is going over to the club. Dougie, too," she added, her face showing exactly how enthusiastic she was about that. "We'll have lunch there and then come back in time to meet Ethan. He's due back around six o'clock. Do you want to come to the club with us?"

"No, thanks," Emma said. "If you're sure you don't need me for anything I'll just stay here and read or something." She didn't add that the last place on earth she wanted to be was the club, where she might run into Kurt. Wouldn't that be fun? She could wish him bon voyage before he jetted off into the sunset with Diana De Witt.

Jane refused to let Emma lift a finger to clean up the breakfast dishes, so she wandered back up to her room and sat forlornly in the window seat, staring out into the distance. So much for work keeping her mind off things. Even the Hewitts didn't seem to want her today. She heaved a sigh. Life seemed utterly miserable. Scenes of Kurt and Diana and Sam and Trent having a grand old time in New York kept playing inside her head.

It just wasn't fair. Emma loved New York. She would have loved to spend some time there with her aunt Liz, her favorite person in the entire world. Emma smiled as she stared out the window, just thinking about her aunt. Liz was her mother's younger sister and was considered the lone eccentric of the family. In her early thirties, unmarried, with a fabulous loft in SoHo, a very hip neighborhood in downtown Manhattan, she had an important job as director of the National Environmental Health Organization. Liz always gave Emma honest, down-to-earth advice. If only Emma could see her, get away for just a little while from all the problems spinning around and around in her head. . . .

A thought struck Emma. Maybe she actually could! She had a standing invitation to visit her aunt. If Liz was home—she traveled a lot—and if Jane could spare Emma for a day or two, she could hop a plane and be in New York in just a few hours. The thought sent her blood racing with excitement. Now that she had thought of the plan, she really, really wanted it to happen.

Emma raced downstairs and caught Jane just as she was running interference between Katie and Wills and Dougie over the train set in the family room.

"Katie can't run the train with us," Wills whined. "She's too little."

"I want to!" Katie screamed.

"You can supervise her and let her run the train once," Jane said to her son. "It would be a nice thing to do."

"Kids," Dougie said, shaking his head with disgust.

"Yeah, kids," Wills echoed, shaking his head, too.

"Excuse me, Jane, could I talk to you?" Emma asked from the doorway.

"Hey, Emma, did you see my train?" Wills asked her eagerly.

"How could I miss it?" Emma laughed. The train and the elaborate tracks reached clear around the room.

"It's not your train, Wills," Jane corrected, heading for the door. "It's the whole family's train."

"Which includes me," Katie said happily, plopping down next to her brother.

"Bogus," Dougie commented.

"Yeah, bogus," Wills agreed.

"Let's sit on the front porch," Jane suggested leading Emma outside. "Honestly, I don't know how much more of Dougie I can take," Jane said with a sigh. "Wills is turning into his little puppet. He's trying so very hard to be ten instead of six."

"Maybe it'll be better when Ethan gets home," Emma said.

"Or worse," Jane commented. "Anyway, what did you want to talk to me about?"

"Well, I was wondering . . . Say no if you don't think this is a good idea."

Jane laughed. "I don't even know what it is yet!"

"Right," Emma agreed. "Well, since you said you don't need me today, I was wondering if you would mind if I took two days off and went to visit my aunt in Manhattan."

Jane looked surprised.

"If it's inconvenient for you, I won't go," Emma added. "I mean, I don't have to go or anything—my job comes first—but I'd like to."

Jane looked pensive for a moment. "Your aunt knows you're coming?"

Emma shook her head. "I haven't called her yet. I wanted to see if it would be okay with you."

"I think so," Jane said slowly. "It seems to me that it will be hard for you to do things, at least until your wrist feels better. And after what you just went through, maybe it would be good for you to get away from the island for a couple of days."

"Really?" Emma asked, jumping up with excitement. "You're sure?"

"I'm sure," Jane answered with a smile. "Let's see, today is Sunday. How about if I expect you back, say, Tuesday afternoon? Sound okay?"

"Oh, that's so great, Jane!" Emma cried, spontaneously squeezing Jane's hand. "I've got to call Liz!" She headed for the front door, then stopped and turned around. "You're sure?" Emma asked. "You don't think I'm shirking my responsibilities or anything?"

"Emma, stop being so perfect!" Jane laughed. "I think Jeff and I are capable of handling our own kids for two days. I would appreciate it if you'd take Dougie with you, though," she added as an afterthought.

Emma ran up the two flights to her room and quickly dialed her aunt's number in New York. "Please be home, please be home," Emma chanted as she paced with the phone.

"Hello?"

"Liz, it's Emma!"

"Hey, stranger! I'm so glad to hear from you!" Liz said happily. "Are you having a wonderful time?"

"Some of it is wonderful, and some of it isn't," Emma said truthfully.

"I know you too well," Liz said. "Something's wrong. I can hear it in your voice."

"So much has been happening," Emma began. "It's just impossible to tell you all about it on the phone. I'd rather talk to you in person. Which leads me to ask . . . if you're up for having a houseguest for two days."

144

"If the guest is you, the answer is always yes," Liz said. "When are you coming?"

"Is today too soon?"

Liz laughed. "I've always liked your decisiveness, Emma. Of course it's okay! Want me to meet your plane?"

"I don't even know what flight I'm taking," Emma said. "I'll just get a cab from the airport. I'll use the extra set of keys you gave me in case you're not there when I arrive."

"Fine, then. I can't wait to see you," Liz said. "I'll clear my schedule, and we'll talk as much as you want."

"Thanks, Liz," Emma said gratefully. "You're sure I'm not intruding?"

"Never," Liz said emphatically. "You just gave me a great excuse to cancel a date with a guy I never should have agreed to go out with in the first place."

"Oh, Liz, you don't have to do that—"

"Are you kidding?" Liz asked. "He was going to take me to his sister's dance recital. I've already sat through two home videos of her in motion. To call it excruciating is kind."

They said good-bye, and Emma quickly called the airline to find out the flight schedule from Bangor to Portland, then from Portland to New York. If she could get to the airport in Bangor in two hours, she could make it. She took out one of her credit cards and quickly booked herself onto both flights.

Emma hung up the phone and went to her closet, trying to decide what to pack. Then she decided not to take anything except her toothbrush and makeup. She and her aunt wore the same size, so she could wear Liz's clothes. Besides, it would be a great excuse to buy some clothes in New York. She felt like indulging herself. No, she deserved to indulge herself! With her left hand, she ran a brush awkwardly through her hair, then grabbed the few things she was taking and headed downstairs.

"I'm leaving now," Emma said to Jane, who was sitting at the kitchen table coloring with Katie.

"You're traveling light," Jane commented when she saw that all Emma carried was her purse.

"It seemed easier. . . . Jane, are you sure you won't need me?" Emma still felt guilty about leaving.

"I'm sure," Jane said. "Don't give it an-other thought. You need a ride to the ferry?"

"I can take the trolley."

"I'll drive you." Jane stood up. "It's no problem. Jeff and Wills and Dougie are currently mesmerized by the train. I promised them another hour of uninterrupted bliss before we leave for the club." She turned to Katie. "How about a ride, little lady?"

"Sally wants to go, too. Is that okay?" Katie said, grabbing her grungy doll.

"Of course Sally can go." Jane picked up her car keys.

"And Dog, too?" Katie added hopefully. Jane hardly ever let Dog ride in the car. He loved it so much that he slobbered all over her, the upholstery, and everything else in sight.

"Dog, too," Jane relented, "although I may live to regret that decision."

Katie scrambled down from her chair to fetch Dog.

They drove quickly to the ferry, Katie chattering happily from her special seat in the back, Dog slobbering all over everything in sight. The ferry was just loading as the car pulled up to the dock.

Emma turned to Jane. "Thanks for the ride," she said softly, "and for giving me the time off."

"Just make sure you come back to us," Jane said. "We'll really miss you."

Emma quickly hugged Katie and Jane then said good-bye and headed for the ferry.

The wind rushed through her hair as she stood on the deck watching Sunset Island fade into the distance. She closed her eyes, reveling in the warmth of the sun on her face and the scent of the sharp, salty air that tickled her nose. For just a moment everything seemed peaceful, perfect. She didn't think about losing Kurt's love or Sam's friendship. For a moment she was free.

TWELVE

It was as if her travel plans were charmed. Both planes arrived on time, and there was no one in the seat next to her in the first-class section on either flight. (This did make Emma think briefly about the fact that she always flew first class and had never actually seen the coach section of an airplane.) There wasn't even a line at the taxi stand at La Guardia Airport, and the cheerful driver did not tell her the story of his life or try to convert her to some obscure religion while driving her to Manhattan. Before Emma knew it, she was ringing the buzzer in her aunt's loft building in SoHo.

"Who is it?" Liz asked through the intercom system.

"Me!" Emma called happily, and her aunt buzzed her in immediately.

"Oh, I'm so glad to see you!" Liz gave Emma a huge hug when she opened her front door. She quickly noticed Emma's bandaged wrist. "What happened to you?"

"It's a long story." Emma stepped inside the loft. "Wow, you put in a hot tub!" she cried, noticing the large redwood tub in the center of the room. "I love it!"

Liz Barrington's loft was a huge open space, formerly some sort of factory, that had been renovated and decorated with her aunt's usual good taste. The floors had been stripped down to the natural wood, and colorful hand-woven rugs here and there marked the living areas. The sparse furnishings were both modern and comfortable. Emma noticed happily that Liz still had the same old couch, an ancient overstuffed piece that her aunt had reupholstered in forest green velvet. It had been Emma's favorite place to read or think since she was a child. Now she ran over to the couch and plopped down, burrowing into the welcoming softness.

"Ahh, home," Emma murmured happily. "Promise me you'll never sell this couch."

"I promise," Liz said. "In fact, it's yours, if you want, as soon as you get your own place."

"Thanks, Liz." Emma snuggled against the cushions. "It's so good to be here."

Liz sat opposite her niece. "No luggage?"

Emma grinned. "You know how much I like your wardrobe."

Liz laughed and walked over to the couch. "You know I never could refuse you anything," Liz said, settling down next to Emma. In old jeans, a T-shirt that read "My Planet, Love it or Leave it", and very little makeup, she looked almost as young as her niece.

"So?" Liz said.

"So," Emma said, "I'm glad to be here."

"I'm glad, too, but you didn't come all the way down here to tell me that."

"No, I didn't," Emma agreed. "I just . . . I really needed to get away for a while."

Liz nodded. "And to spill your guts."

"I've been having a few problems," Emma agreed tentatively. "It's hard to talk about them."

"You know you don't have to tell me anything unless you want to," Liz reminded her. "I was just teasing you."

"I want to tell you," Emma said earnestly. "God, Liz, I'm so confused. . . ."

Her aunt listened sympathetically as

151

Emma told her the story of her summer on the island. She didn't leave anything out. By the time she finished talking she had told Liz all about her friendship with Carrie and Sam, about Lorell and Diana and Daphne, including the horrible story about Daphne attacking her, about lying to everyone about how rich she was, and all about Kurt.

"And that's the whole awful story," Emma finally concluded. She glanced out the window and noticed it was getting dark. "Oh, Liz, I'm sorry! I've been talking forever!"

"Quite a saga," Liz said, stretching her legs. She looked pensive for a moment. "Listen, I'm starved. How about I nuke some leftover Chinese food in the microwave while I try to think of something incredibly wise to tell you?"

"The way I see it," Liz said half an hour later as she lifted some lemon chicken to her mouth with chopsticks, "you feel betrayed by both Kurt and Sam. Is that right?"

"Right," Emma agreed eagerly. "But they don't see it that way. Not at all."

"I'm sure they don't. If they agreed with you they wouldn't be doing what they're doing, right?"

152

"Right," Emma echoed firmly. "I'm so glad you agree with me, Liz. I knew I was right!"

"Well, you're not, really," Liz said, "at least not completely. More shrimp?"

Emma shook her head impatiently. "What do you mean?" she demanded.

Liz served herself some more butterfly shrimp and looked thoughtful. "Well, it seems to me that just because someone is your friend doesn't mean you have to approve of every decision that friend makes. I'm talking about Sam here," Liz said.

"But Sam hates those girls!" Emma protested. "I just can't understand why she would go to a concert with them."

"I don't know how hard you've tried to understand, really," Liz said.

"I did try," Emma insisted, putting down her chopsticks. She did not like the way this was going at all.

"You've never not had money, Emma," Liz reminded her niece gently. "Think about it. Sam sounds like a bright, funny, wonderful girl. She wants to have adventures she's never had. You've had so many more opportunities than she has!"

"I guess," Emma said, looking down at her plate.

"So what if she's temporarily seduced by Trent's money? People go out with people for all kinds of reasons." Liz shrugged. "If Sam is the kind of girl you say she is, she won't lose sight of what's really important or who her real friends are. You have to have a little faith in her. That's part of being her friend."

Emma looked forlorn. "I really messed that up, huh?"

Liz smiled. "Oh, Em, you didn't mess anything up. Everyone makes mistakes—I make tons of them. You have always been very, very hard on yourself, you know."

"Am I wrong about Kurt, too?" Emma asked in a small voice.

"That's a tougher question, and I'm afraid it's one you're going to have to figure out yourself."

"But I can't figure it out!" Emma protested. "He broke my heart, and he doesn't even seem to care!"

"It sounds to me as if he does care," Liz said. "But it also sounds as if he's not really ready for the kind of intense romance you envisioned."

"I thought he was perfect," Emma admitted. "I thought he was different from other men, not like Daddy or Austin. I thought he would never hurt me."

"Oh, sweetheart, it's very hard to find a twenty-year-old boy who will never hurt you," Liz said. "He doesn't even know who he is yet. Sometimes in learning who he is, he ends up hurting you."

"And getting involved with Diana is part of figuring out who he is?" Emma asked.

"It might be."

"Then he's not the person I thought he was," Emma said sadly.

"Maybe not," Liz agreed. "But the important thing is that you're becoming the person you want to be."

Emma wandered over to the couch and plopped back down on the cushions. "It doesn't feel important, Liz. It feels awful."

Liz laughed. "I know. But notice I refrained from calling it a 'learning experience.' People always use that horrible phrase when what they really mean is that everything went wrong and life sucks."

Emma smiled wryly. "I'll have that silk-screened on a T-shirt: 'Everything went wrong and life sucks.' It'll be my new motto."

"Listen, enough of this wise-old-Liz stuff,"

Emma's aunt said. "I don't know about you, but I'm still hungry. How about if we walk down to the ice cream place on the corner. The butter pecan is to die for."

They went for ice cream, and then took a walk around SoHo. Liz told Emma all about her job and the guys she was dating. When they got back to the loft they put on bathing suits and sat in the hot tub for a while, Emma's injured arm dangling over the side. Emma could feel the tension leaving her body, and the next thing she knew her aunt was shaking her awake.

"Better get out. You're starting to look kind of pruney," Liz said, helping Emma out of the hot tub.

Emma pulled off the wet bathing suit, put on a T-shirt, and was asleep on the couch before she could wash her face or brush her teeth. It was the most relaxing sleep she'd had in a long time.

Emma woke up first in the morning. She showered and changed the bandage on her wrist, using the supplies she had tucked into her purse, then pulled some jeans and a T-shirt out of her aunt's dresser.

By the time Liz crawled out of bed, Emma

had eggs, croissants, and hot coffee on the table that faced the large window.

"You certainly look better," Liz commented as she sat down at the table.

"I feel better." Emma poured Liz some coffee.

"Come to any conclusions?"

"Not really," Emma admitted. "But I don't feel quite so—I don't know—overwhelmed by everything."

"Well, that's a good start. So what do you want to do today? Museums? Shopping?"

"Nothing that involves my mind," Emma said, making a face. "My brain has been on overdrive."

"Okay, then, shopping," Liz decided. "Fun-type shopping, not Kat-type shopping," she added.

Emma laughed. She knew exactly what her aunt meant. To Emma's mom, Kat, shopping was very serious business. It involved getting dressed to kill—perfect hair, perfect nails, perfect makeup—and keeping appointments with couturiers. Emma had been shopping that way since she was four years old.

"Fun-type shopping where?" Emma asked eagerly.

"The East Village," Liz decreed, sipping her coffee. "Serious spandex, leather bras, a barbershop where they razor cut your initials into your hair."

Emma laughed. "Can I skip the razor cut?"

Liz sighed with mock gravity. "You never did understand style, dear."

They cleaned up the kitchen area quickly and set out into the bright morning sunshine, heading for the East Village. As they walked north, the streets of SoHo and the Village were like another country. At an outdoor café three skinheads—one female—in army fatigues sat sipping espresso, their guitar cases lying beside them. One beat drumsticks on the small table as he read over some sheet music. They walked past a tiny store whose window displayed Barbie dolls with green hair wearing black leather hot pants. A large white sculpture of what looked like a mother and child was being hoisted up with a rope and pulleys to a fourth-floor loft. The four men working on the project were arguing loudly in Italian about how to accomplish the job. Emma stopped for a minute on a corner where a young violinist played a haunting melody.

His violin case lay open before him on the sidewalk, bearing a sign that read "Help me stay in Juilliard." Emma pulled a ten dollar bill out of her wallet and dropped it into the violin case. A homeless man saw this and stood in front of Emma with his hand out. "I'm hungry," he said. Emma pulled out another ten dollar bill, leaving the homeless man calling out "God bless you" over and over and she and Liz walked away.

"Easy to tell you're not a New Yorker," Liz said as they walked east through Washington Square Park.

"Because I gave them money?" Emma asked. "Don't you?"

"Sometimes," Liz admitted. "But you could spend all day every day just handing people money in this city, and it wouldn't make a particle of difference."

"It might to the people you give the money to," Emma said, dodging a running dog.

"Maybe," Liz conceded, "for an hour or even a day. But the whole system needs to be changed. Oh, listen, don't let me climb up on my soapbox!"

"I want to know what you think," Emma assured her.

"Well, I like to think my job helps change things," Liz said thoughtfully. "And I work in a soup kitchen at a women's shelter once a week when I'm in town."

"So you give of yourself in addition to giving money," Emma said.

"Right," Liz agreed. "I mean, we have money, so I think we have a responsibility to do both."

Emma nodded. Her parents gave to a variety of charities, mostly those that were dear to the hearts of the Beautiful People, such as the ballet. She could just imagine Kat Cresswell volunteering to work in a soup kitchen. A laughable thought.

They reached the east side of the park and listened for a moment to two girls playing guitars and singing an old Beatles song.

"Once you told me you'd thought about joining the Peace Corps," Liz said as they started walking again.

Emma nodded. Liz was the only person she had ever told her secret dream to, until this summer, when she'd blurted it out to Kurt. He'd been so impressed that she'd felt guilty, as if she had said it only to sound like a kind of girl he would like.

The truth was that Emma wasn't sure if

she was serious about it or not. She had come to New York during Christmas vacation last year, and Liz had taken her to a party, where she met a bunch of former Peace Corps members. Emma thought they were the nicest, most interesting people she'd ever met. One young man in particular had made a real impact on her. He'd spent two years in Africa. He'd shown videos at the party of some of his students and of a school he'd helped build. He had made a tremendous impression on Emma, as had his friends. She'd started thinking that perhaps she could find some answers, some meaning in her life, if she joined the Peace Corps.

"Are you still thinking about it?" Liz asked.

Emma nodded. She thought about the literature she'd sent away for and about the application form that lay in the bottom of her desk drawer at home in Boston. She tried to imagine telling her parents that she was joining the Peace Corps. They would think she had totally lost her mind.

"Well, if you ever want to talk with Charlie about it, I'll set it up," Liz said. Charlie was her friend who had been in Africa. "No hurry. Whenever you want, *if* you want," she added.

"Thanks," Emma said. "Right now I can't even get my summer right, much less figure out what to do with the rest of my life."

"Ah, the East Village," Liz said as they hit Astor Place. "The only neighborhood where you can find sidewalk vendors selling pink ceramic flamingos."

Sure enough, displayed on a blanket amid used books, old magazines, and even older clothes were two chipped pink flamingos designed to be stuck into one's front lawn.

"But nobody in Manhattan has a front lawn!" Emma whispered to her aunt.

"That's why you can get a bargain on them!" Liz laughed.

They wandered in and out of stores along the side streets, occasionally trying on clothes, the more outlandish the better. Because of Emma's injured wrist, Liz had to help her in and out of things, which had them both giggling hysterically in the dressing rooms. In a shop called Killer Klothes a woman with a green Mohawk haircut and a ring through her nose waited on them. She looked mad at the world and kept ripping the T-shirt she was wearing. Emma bought lime green biking pants with a lime green and black polka-dot bare-midriff top, pointy-toed white lace ankle boots, and red sun-glasses shaped like two hearts.

"Aren't you somebody?" the salesgirl asked grumpily as she rang up Emma's purchases.

"Somebody?" Emma asked.

"Yeah, I saw you in that slasher flick, *Zombie High.* You bought it on a water bed," the girl said. "I'm an actress, too," she added sullenly.

"Isn't everybody?" Liz asked lightly.

"I could have died better than you did," the girl mumbled, ripping more holes in her T-shirt.

"Weird. Very weird," Liz said when they got outside.

"I was brilliant in that movie, wasn't I, darling?" Emma giggled, donning her new sunglasses.

"I thought you died artfully," Liz agreed.

"You know what?" Emma turned impetu-ously to her aunt. "I want to get Sam a present. Sort of a let's-make-up present. What do you think?"

"Good idea," Liz agreed.

"Let's see . . . not too expensive, so she doesn't think I'm showing off. . . . I know! A T-shirt! A really funny personalized one!"

Emma said, spying a T-shirt store across the street. "Let's think of something great for them to put on it," Emma said as they dodged a convertible blaring a Garth Brooks tape.

"How about 'Rich or poor, it's nice to have money,'" Liz suggested.

"Oh, very funny." Emma pushed open the door to the store. "Wait! I have an idea! How about . . ."

Emma's suggestion died on her lips—because there in front of her stood Kurt Ackerman and Diana De Witt. Her mind took in the scene before her—Kurt with his arm around a laughing Diana De Witt, who was wearing a T-shirt bearing the unmistakable computer image of a grinning Kurt Ackerman.

THIRTEEN

A silent plea went through Emma's head as she stood facing Kurt and Diana, unable to move or speak: *Please, God, let a big hole appear in the floor so that I can fall through right now.*

"Well, hi there!" Diana greeted Emma with a malicious smile. She snuggled closer to Kurt. "Imagine running into you in New York!"

"Imagine," Emma echoed numbly.

Diana leaned closer to Emma and spoke confidentially. "You know, frankly, I'm surprised that you'd want to spy on us so badly that you'd follow us all the way here. It's kind of . . . pathetic, isn't it?"

Emma's face burned with embarrassment. "I did not follow you," she said, keeping her eyes on Diana so that she wouldn't have to look at Kurt. "I came to visit my aunt. We're shopping."

Liz gave a little wave at Diana and Kurt. "I'm the aunt," she said. Then she excused herself and crossed to the other side of the store, feigning interest in some T-shirts displayed on the wall.

Kurt dropped his arm from Diana's waist and ran his hand nervously through his hair. "This is really low, Emma," he said.

Emma stared at him incredulously. "You don't actually believe I followed you, do you?"

"You're here, aren't you?" Kurt said. "What, are you going to tell me this is a coincidence?"

"Yes, that's exactly what it is," Emma said. She looked from Kurt's belligerent, chagrined face to Diana's smug expression. "You two really deserve each other," she said bitterly. This was not the Kurt Ackerman she had fallen in love with. This was someone she didn't even like. Diana De Witt was welcome to him!

"Come on, Kurt," Diana said, taking his hand and coaxing him toward the door. "Let's go back and buy those matching satin baseball jackets we saw next door."

Kurt allowed Diana to lead him, as if he had no mind of his own. He turned away from Emma, but Diana looked back at her once they reached the door. "Bye-bye, Emma!" she called cheerfully. "Maybe Kurt and I will see you back on the island sometime."

Emma stood rooted to the spot. Three young kids had to walk around her, giving her weird looks, which she barely noticed.

"I take it that was Kurt and Diana," Liz said.

Emma nodded mutely.

"And I take it seeing them was excruciating."

Emma nodded again.

"This is one of those awful coincidences that people think only happen in books." Liz looked sympathetic.

"They think I followed them here to spy on them," Emma whispered.

"That's obnoxious," Liz said, "not to mention egocentric."

"They'll tell everyone on the island that I followed them," Emma continued. "As soon as they rejoin Lorell and the others, they'll tell them, and the story will spread like wildfire," Emma continued in a daze. "No one will believe that I just happened to come to New York and I just happened to run into them."

"So?" Liz asked.

Emma turned on her aunt. "What do you mean 'so'? *So* I will be the laughingstock of Sunset Island."

"Well, if you're really concerned about that, you're just as egocentric and self-involved as they are," Liz said mildly.

"You don't understand at all!" Emma cried.

"Oh, Em, I do, too," Liz said. "I know you feel embarrassed and hurt. But in the scheme of things, this coincidence is not important." Liz caught sight of two people standing outside the display window of the store—a young woman in rags holding a little girl by the hand. As the skinny little girl stared up at her mother's pleading face, the woman asked everyone who left the store for money. "That," Liz said emphatically, pointing to the woman, "is important. And you're old enough to start getting your priorities straight."

Emma was staring out the window when Diana and Kurt walked by hand in hand, looking as if they didn't have a care in the world. The woman who was begging approached them with her hand out. Diana and Kurt passed her by without breaking stride.

"I wish I could make the world over into the place I want it to be," Emma said sadly.

Liz put her arm around Emma's shoulders and gave her a quick hug. "So do I, Em. So do I."

That night and the next morning Emma walked miles through SoHo, sometimes with Liz and sometimes by herself. The anonymity of the teeming streets appealed to her. She felt melancholy and confused. It seemed as if there were no clear solutions to her problems, and although she was bitterly disappointed in Kurt, she couldn't seem to loosen his hold on her heart.

Liz insisted on riding with Emma in the taxi to the airport, so that she could spend as much time with her niece as possible. "I hope you found what you were looking for," she said, hugging Emma in front of the airline terminal.

"I don't know," Emma said with a sad smile. "I didn't even realize I was looking." She hugged her aunt harder. "But thank you. It was wonderful to be here, to see you."

"Think of my place as home," Liz said simply.

Emma hugged her aunt again and headed for her departure gate.

Once again the flight was right on time, and Emma settled down in the first-class section of the plane. As she skimmed a fashion magazine, an article caught her eyes: "Poor, Dirty, and Underpaid—The Happiest Year of My Life." The article was written by a young woman who had spent a year in the Peace Corps living in Swaziland. Emma was fascinated by the story and read it avidly. The accompanying photos showed the author teaching the native children, taking part in a tribal ceremony, and helping to dig a well. *Maybe that could be me,* Emma thought, studying the photos. *Yeah, and maybe as soon as I left money and privilege behind I'd be a sniveling little wreck,* she added to herself. But how would she ever know, unless she was willing to test herself? Test herself . . . and risk failing.

It was early evening by the time Emma got back to the Hewitts'. She was greeted at the front door by an overjoyed Katie, who threw her arms around Emma and exclaimed, "My Emma's back!"

"Hi, there!" Jane called from the kitchen when she saw Emma in the hall. "Come on in! We missed you!"

The entire family, including Dougie, had gathered in the kitchen. Emma felt a rush of gratitude to be a part of this noisy, boisterous group.

Jane gave Emma a hug. "You're just in time for dinner—my infamous spaghetti."

"Did you have fun?" Jeff asked as he and the younger boys set the table.

"It was great," Emma said.

Ethan was sitting at the table playing a miniature computer game. "Score!" he yelled triumphantly.

Emma grinned at him. His hair had turned an even brighter red from his days outside camping. "Hi there, stranger," she said, ruffling his hair. "How was your trip?"

"Awesome." Ethan didn't even look up from the computer game. "I won five bucks on this baby. I beat everyone at camp!"

"So much for learning to rub two sticks together to start a fire," Jeff said wryly.

"Challenge ya," Dougie said, casually

looking over Ethan's shoulder as he manipulated the computer game.

"You any good?" Ethan asked.

"I'm okay," Dougie said.

"After dinner," Jeff said. "Ethan, stop playing and help your brother carry the food to the table."

"Score!" Ethan yelled.

"Put it away, Ethan. Now!" Jeff had worked his way up to his no-nonsense voice. Ethan reluctantly put the computer down.

"So, we on for after dinner?" Dougie asked Ethan as he carried the garlic bread to the table.

"Sure," Ethan said casually. "I'll give you a shot."

"But after dinner we're supposed to run the train," Wills reminded the older boys. "Dad said."

"So?" Ethan asked, looking coolly at his little brother.

"Yeah, so?" Dougie added.

Wills couldn't seem to think of an answer. Emma saw the anxiety etched on his face. It appeared that Dougie was now becoming Ethan's friend and ignoring Wills.

"We can do the train, too," Jeff assured his younger son.

Emma washed quickly and joined them all at the large dinner table. Everyone dug into Jane's famous spaghetti while Ethan regaled them with stories about his camping trip. "So Stuey feels something in his sleeping bag," Ethan continued, "and he starts yelling, 'You guys, something is in here,' but Stuey is such a wuss that we don't believe him. Anyhow, finally Timmy Martin turns a flashlight on, just to shut Stuey up, and there's this monster snake slithering around in Stuey's sleeping bag!"

"What did you do?" Dougie asked, wide-eyed.

"Stuey's jumping around like he peed his pants," Ethan said, laughing, "so I just took a stick and, like, pushed the snake away. No biggie."

"Cool," Dougie breathed.

"You're probably the one who peed his pants," Wills muttered. "You think you're so big."

Ethan slurped some spaghetti from his fork. He gave his little brother a superior look. "I will always be bigger than you," he said loftily.

"Ethan, you are being obnoxious," Jane said, then sipped her iced tea.

"Who am I bigger than?" Katie asked around a mouthful of spaghetti.

"Bigger is not important," Jeff said. "People have no control over how big they are."

"He only says that because he's the biggest one in the family," Ethan commented smugly.

The phone rang, and Jeff got up to answer it. He came back to the table just as Ethan was finishing yet another story about scout camp.

"That was Brent," Jeff said to his wife as he sat down. Brent was a young lawyer in Hewitts' firm. "He says Louis Freeman is screaming about the will, and he wants to see both of us tonight or he'll pull his account."

"Again?" Jane sighed.

Jane and Jeff were the lawyers for the Freeman family, whose wealth was almost as great as that of Emma's family's. Louis Freeman had recently married a woman thirty years younger then he, and his family was furious because he had changed his will. He wanted—demanded—personal attention from Jeff and Jane Hewitt.

"If we're lucky, we can settle the problem this week," Jeff said. He turned to Wills.

"Your mom and I have to go to the office for a couple of hours."

"But what about the train?" Wills whined.

"Tell you what. Tomorrow we'll spend the whole day together, just you and Ethan and me. We'll run the train and do whatever else you guys want."

"Okay," Wills said reluctantly. He knew his dad almost always kept his word.

"You okay to stay with the kids, Emma?" Jane asked as she stood up to clear the table.

"Oh, sure," Emma said, getting up to help. "No problem."

"I didn't want to play trains, anyway," Ethan said.

"Me, neither," Dougie said.

Emma knew this cut Wills to the quick. He and Dougie had spent hours and hours setting up the train system. Now Dougie was turning traitor.

Emma organized the kids into assisting her with the dinner cleanup as Jane and Jeff got ready to leave. She turned the dishwasher on, and Ethan went out to the back patio with his computer game, Dougie close behind.

"Want to play Barbies?" Katie asked Wills hopefully.

"Shut up!" Wills yelled at her. "You're just a stupid baby!"

Katie's bottom lip quivered. She loved Wills. He never yelled at her.

"Score!" Ethan yelled from the patio.

"Sorry," Wills mumbled. Then he marched out of the kitchen, ran upstairs to his room, and slammed the door behind him.

"Is he mad at me?" Katie asked Emma. In search of comfort she grabbed her doll, Sally, off a chair.

"No, honey, he's not mad," Emma said, kneeling to hug Katie.

"Score!" Ethan crowed again.

Emma made a decision.

"How about we shoot some baskets when you guys finish your game?" she asked Ethan and Dougie from inside the sliding glass door to the patio.

"I'm on Ethan's team," Dougie said quickly.

"How about the winner of the computer game is captain of one team and the loser is captain of the other team?" Emma suggested. "Winner gets first pick."

"Sure," Ethan said, not looking up from the computer.

"Good, we'll be waiting for you." Emma

went upstairs to tell Wills. She knew he was pretty good at shooting baskets. Emma herself was horrible. Wills would undoubtedly be the first person chosen by whoever won the computer contest.

It didn't take long for Dougie to lose, and everyone met at the hoop on the garage.

"Okay, Ethan, you're the winner," Emma said. "Pick your team."

"Dougie," he said, bouncing the basketball once.

Wills scowled and kicked a stone across the driveway.

"You can't pick Dougie," Emma said reasonably. "That was the rule." She wanted to pick Ethan up and shake him for being so obnoxious to Wills.

Ethan groaned melodramatically. "Okay, I'll take . . . Wills." He said it as if his brother were being forced on him. Wills moved reluctantly toward Ethan.

"I'll take Emma," Dougie said.

"And Katie," Emma added. "We're a package deal."

"Winning team shoots first," Ethan said, dribbling the ball. "Point for every basket. Keep the ball till your team misses. First team with twenty points is the winner." He explained the house rules for Dougie's benefit.

"And I get help because I'm little," Katie added seriously.

Ethan made a basket, then passed the ball to Wills, who dribbled once, shot, and missed.

"Figures," Ethan said under his breath. Wills blushed and passed the ball to Dougie.

Dougie dribbled around the driveway yelling like a sports commentator. "He stops, he shoots—*yes!*" he crowed as the ball sailed into the basket. He cupped his hands around his mouth and made a whooshing noise. "And the crowd goes wild!" he yelled. He passed the ball to Emma. To her surprise she made a basket. Then she lifted Katie high up in her arms, and the little girl threw the ball. With an assist from Dougie the ball tipped into the basket.

"Did you see me?" Katie cried excitedly. "I made a basket!"

It was Dougie's turn again, but this time he missed, so the ball went back to Ethan. He put one in and passed the ball to Wills. "Don't mess up," Ethan warned him.

Wills was visibly nervous. He dribbled twice, shot, and missed by a mile.

178

"You are so stupid!" Ethan yelled at his little brother. "Katie plays better than you do!"

Just as Wills caught the ball, Ethan turned away from him in disgust. Wills was so mad at his brother that before Emma could open her mouth to say anything, he had heaved the basketball as hard as he could at Ethan's back.

Just at the moment Ethan turned around. The ball that was meant for his back smacked him hard in the nose.

"My nose!" Ethan screamed, pressing his hands to his face. To everyone's horror, blood dripped out from between his fingers.

Emma ran to him. "Let me see," she demanded, gently pulling his hands away from his face. His nose seemed to be crooked, and it was rapidly turning blue. "I think it's broken," Emma said. "We're going to the clinic emergency room. Just stay right there, Ethan," she instructed. "I'll get the car keys." She turned around to tell the other kids to get into the car, but only Katie and Dougie were standing there. Wills was gone.

FOURTEEN

Emma left Ethan on the front porch with ice on his nose and ran around the Hewitts' property, calling and looking everywhere she could think of. No Wills. She quickly ran next door to the Steins' house. Stinky Stein was Wills's best friend.

"Is Wills here?" Emma asked breathlessly when Stuey Stein opened the door.

"Uh-uh," Stuey said between bites of pizza.

"Where's Stinky?" Emma asked.

"He went to the movies with my parents."

From behind Stuey came Brenda Clauser, a wild thirteen-year-old girl who did a lot of baby-sitting on the island. "Hi," she said. "I'm the sitter." She took a bite of her slice of pizza and let some of the tomato sauce fall on

180

the white hall carpet. "Oops," she said mildly, making no move to clean it up.

"If you see Wills, will you call me right away?" Emma asked.

"Did he run away?" Stuey asked.

"Just call me if you see him."

Emma dashed back to the Hewitts' house. The sky was getting darker. Ethan's nose was getting bluer. And Wills was still missing. Ethan, Dougie, Katie all stared at her, waiting to see what she would do.

"Just hold the ice against your nose, Ethan," Emma instructed. "I'll be right back." She ran inside and quickly dialed the Templetons' number.

The phone rang four times, and then a recording came on saying that no one was home. "Great, just great," Emma muttered under her breath. She hung up and dialed Mr. Jacobs's number. "Please be home, please be home," Emma chanted as she paced with the phone.

"Jacobs residence," came Sam's voice.

"Sam! Oh, I'm so glad you're back! It's Emma."

Sam apparently heard the frenzy in Emma's voice and put aside all thoughts of their fight. "What's wrong?" she asked quickly.

Emma rapidly explained what had happened. "I've looked everywhere for Wills—but no luck," she finished. "I can't leave here until I find him. It's getting dark out. Can you take Ethan to the emergency room at the clinic?"

"Yeah, we're in luck. The monsters are out with their dad," Sam said. "I'm on my way."

Emma ran back to the kids on the front porch. "Okay, Ethan, Sam is on her way here to take you to the clinic," she assured him.

Sam made it across the island in record time and pulled into the Hewitts' driveway with a screech of tires.

"Your chariot awaits," she said as she gently helped Ethan into the front seat.

"Thanks a million," Emma called to Sam as she pulled out of the driveway.

Katie stuck Sally's arm in her mouth, a sure sign that she was anxious. "Is Wills scared?" she asked.

"I think so, honey," Emma said.

"It wasn't Wills's fault," Dougie said quickly.

Oh, great, Emma thought. *Now* he defends Wills. She turned to Dougie. "Can you think of anywhere he might have gone?"

182

Dougie shook his head.

"Think, Dougie!" Emma practically screamed. "You've spent every second with him for the past week. Where would he go to hide?"

Dougie started to shrug, but then his face changed. "Wait a minute. The fort!"

"You and Wills have a fort?" Emma asked eagerly. "Where is it?"

Dougie's face clouded over. "I'm not supposed to tell. It's a secret. We spit on it."

Emma was about ready to pick Dougie up and shake him until she rattled the information out of him. She took a deep breath and forced herself to speak calmly and authoritatively. "Dougie, you must tell me where the fort is. Wills could get hurt there in the dark, all by himself."

"Well, these kids from the club, they dug this fort by the trees near the private beach," Dougie explained reluctantly.

"Did you say 'dug'?" Emma asked.

Dougie nodded. "It's underground. They'll murdelize me for telling."

"*I* will murdelize you here and now if you don't show me where it is," Emma threatened him. Out of the corner of her eye she saw the Steins' car pull into their driveway.

"You wait right here," she told Dougie. "Don't move."

Emma dashed back over to the house next door. She explained the situation to an astonished Trina and Stanley Stein. "So can you please watch Katie and the house?" Emma asked. "I've got to go look for this underground fort with Dougie."

Stinky Stein listened with his mouth hanging open. "Not the underground fort!" he cried. "The older kids said no one should use it anymore, because one part is caving in!"

Emma's heart constricted with fear.

"I'll stay at the Hewitts' while you're gone," Trina assured Emma. "Don't worry."

"Maybe you should call the police," Stanley Stein suggested.

"If I don't find him soon, I will," Emma said, and ran back to the Hewitts', Trina right beside her.

"Let's go, Dougie," Emma said, pulling Dougie into the car.

She drove quickly and silently to the club.

"Over that way," Dougie directed when they got there. Emma drove behind the clubhouse to a little-used parking area by a large wooded area near the private beach.

Emma followed Dougie through the trees, stumbling around in the dark. She cursed herself for not bringing a flashlight.

"Which way, Dougie?" Emma asked, when they were inside the woodsy area, trees all around them.

Dougie looked confused. "I can't tell. It's too dark."

Emma was about to yell at Dougie. There had to be some landmark, some way to tell which way to go, but as she stared at the menacing branches surrounding them, she realized that there really was no way to tell one direction from another. She wasn't even sure which way it was back to the car. Great. Now she'd managed to get herself and Dougie lost, too.

"We're going to start calling for him," Emma told Dougie, "as loud as we can. Wills!" she shouted.

"Wills!" Dougie screamed.

"Wills, it's Emma!" she yelled at the top of her lungs. "Can you hear me?"

She listened attentively for a second. There was no answer. She made a small turn and cupped her hands around her mouth. "Wills!" she screamed. "Wills!"

What was that? Had she heard a noise?

"Hey, I thought I heard—" Dougie began.

"Shhh!" Emma instructed Dougie quickly. "Wills!" she yelled again.

Yes! She did hear something!

"Emma?" came a tiny voice in the distance.

"I'm here, Wills!" Emma called, turning in the direction of the voice. "Don't move! I'm coming!"

Emma ran toward Wills's voice. "Call again, Wills, so I can follow your voice!"

"I'm here!"

"Keep calling!" Emma yelled.

"I'm here! I'm here!" Wills kept calling as Emma and Dougie moved closer and closer. Emma pushed through some thick branches that opened into a small clearing, and there was Wills, sitting next to a big hole marked with a small American flag.

"Oh, Wills!" Emma cried, running to put her arms around the little boy. His face was dirty and streaked with tears. Emma hugged him as hard as she could. "I was so worried! Oh, thank God you're all right!"

"Did you go in the fort?" Dougie asked Wills.

Wills shook his head and sniffed back the last of his tears. "I was going to," he said. "I ran all the way here. But then I remembered Kevin Nucomb said that you always had to test the fort first, to make sure there wasn't a cave-in. So I threw a big rock in the dirt over there where the secret room is."

Emma looked around her. She couldn't see any big rock. "Where did the rock go?"

"There," Wills said, pointing to a second large hole farther away. "It caved in," he added in a scared voice.

"Oh, Wills, you were so smart to remember to check!" Emma exclaimed, hugging Wills again. A chill ran down her spine. If Wills had crawled into the underground fort he could have been buried alive.

Wills looked shyly at Dougie, who was examining the hole where the cave-in had occurred. "Awesome," Dougie announced. "You were megabrave, Wills."

"Yeah?" Will said. It was as if the sun had come out to shine on his face. Then he realized how uncool he was acting. "No biggie," he added nonchalantly, sounding exactly like Ethan.

"Wills, do you know the way back to the parking lot?" Emma asked. She had little hope that he actually would.

Wills looked around for a second, then up at the sky. "That way," he said, pointing.

Emma was surprised. "How do you know?"

"Dad taught me to look for the North Star," he explained. "It was behind me on my way here. And I remember passing that white tree."

Sure enough, Emma noticed a white birch. There was only one. Taking Wills's advice they followed the North Star and the white tree, and soon Emma could use the lights from the club in the far distance to guide them the rest of the way.

The lights were burning brightly in the Hewitts' house when Emma pulled into the driveway. Trina Stein, Sam, Ethan, and Katie met them at the front door. Ethan's nose was covered with a bandage.

"Oh, Wills!" Katie cried, happily throwing her arms around her brother.

"Hi," Ethan said carefully.

"Hi," Wills said.

Emma told them what had happened. "Wills was smart and brave," she said, her arm around his shoulders. "And if it hadn't been for him, we might all still be lost in the woods."

"I'm glad you're okay," Ethan said, not looking Wills in the eye.

"I'm glad you're okay, too," Trina Stein said, ruffling Wills's hair. "I'll be going. Oh, Dougie, your mom called. She said you're to come right home."

"I'll call and see if I can spend the night," Dougie said eagerly, going for the phone.

"Wait a second, Dougie," Emma said. "I think you'd better go home tonight. The boys will see you soon."

"Aw, gee," Dougie griped, "nothing exciting ever happens at my house. People over here are always getting wrecked or something!"

Emma ushered Dougie out the door and watched him run to his own house.

Ethan and Wills went upstairs, Emma and Sam sat on the couch, and Katie snuggled up sleepily in Emma's lap.

"I'm exhausted," Emma said, letting her head fall back on the couch. Had she really been in New York just this morning? It seemed like eons ago. "Is Ethan okay?" she asked Sam.

"His nose is broken," Sam said. "The doctor gave him a painkiller, and I got the prescription filled on the way home." She pulled a medicine bottle out of her purse and handed it to Emma.

"That's funny," Emma said, studying the labels. "This is the same medication I've got upstairs for my wrist."

"Ethan was quite the little trooper," Sam said. "And he's very single-minded. I know the pain pill must be knocking him out, but he absolutely insisted on staying awake to make sure Wills was okay."

Emma stroked Katie's hair thoughtfully and shook her head. "Kids . . . they're unbelievable. I know how much Ethan loves Wills, but sometimes he's just so hateful to him. Do brothers and sisters always act this way?" asked Emma. "I'm an only child—I have no frame of reference."

"Well, my mother insists that when Ruth Anne was a baby I once tried to drop her out a second-story window," Sam said, "so maybe they do." Ruth Anne was Sam's sixteen-year-old sister.

"Do you love Ruth Anne?" Emma asked.

"She's a pain in the ass and a total suck-up, and sometimes I can't stand her. But yeah, I love her," Sam added nonchalantly.

Emma smiled down at Katie's sleepy face. "I guess I'd better put this little girl to bed." She stood up with Katie in her arms. "I can't thank you enough for taking Ethan to the clinic."

Sam waved away the thanks. "That's what friends are for. Besides, the doctor was rather hunky."

Emma laughed. "Trust you to find a guy-opportunity in the most dire circumstances." She hoisted Katie in her arms, taking care not to hurt her bandaged wrist. "How was your trip?" she asked carefully.

"Fun," Sam said. "I mean, being in New York again was the fun part," she added quickly. "I wish I could have gone with you and Carrie, though," she added. "New York would never be the same."

They started walking toward the stairs.

"Everything was okay with Trent?" Emma asked.

Sam shrugged. "If you mean did he force himself on me or anything gross like that, the answer is no. He's easily deterred, frankly."

Emma laughed. "I always thought so, too." She looked down at Katie for a moment, then back at Sam. "I was wrong to get so mad about your going."

"Well, thanks for that." Sam smiled. "I hope you don't think I'm going to start hanging out with Lorell and Diana or anything," she added. "They are not my idea of a good time."

"This little girl is getting heavy," Emma said, sitting on the bottom step with Katie sound asleep in her lap.

"Lorell and Diana are just . . . unbelievable," Sam continued, shaking her head. "Every sentence they utter seems to begin with the 'I' word. They couldn't care less about anyone else. Daphne was supposed to go on this trip, but once they found out she was in the hospital they just shrugged it off. I mean, they never even talked about her or how sick she is or how they'd go and visit her. They just didn't even seem to care."

"Maybe they don't," Emma said.

"Maybe," Sam agreed. "I'm just glad my friends aren't like that," she added. She and Emma stared at each other for a moment. Then they both broke into smiles. Everything between them was going to be all right.

After Sam drove off into the night, Emma carried Katie upstairs. She thought about Sam and how hard she'd been on their friendship. There was time enough later to explain to Sam why she'd been in New York. There was time enough to talk about Trent and Sam and who might be using whom. Emma was just glad their fight was over.

"Okay, little one," Emma whispered, laying Katie down in her bed. Trina had obviously given Katie her bath and helped her change into pink pajamas. Emma kissed Katie and tiptoed out of the room.

She peeked into Ethan's room. He was sound asleep, his bandaged nose shining in the hall light. Emma gently shut his bedroom door.

She found Wills sitting on his bed, holding a teddy bear that Jane told her had been his constant companion when he was an infant.

"Quite an evening," Emma said quietly, sitting down on his bed.

Wills shrugged and held his bear tighter.

"Did you and Ethan talk?" Emma asked.

"Yep," Wills said. "He told me he was glad I wasn't dead."

"He said that because he was scared when you ran away," Emma explained. "Ethan really cares about you."

"No, he doesn't," Wills said.

"Oh, yes, honey, he does!" Emma told him. "So many people do! Me and your parents and Katie and Ethan and Dougie—"

"Dougie doesn't care about me," Wills said, looking down at his bear. "He's Ethan's friend now. I hate him. And I hate Ethan,

193

too." Wills's lower lip was starting to tremble. He was making a valiant effort not to cry.

"It must have made you really mad when Ethan came home and Dougie started paying a lot of attention to him," Emma said softly, searching for the right words to say.

"He's supposed to be my friend!" Wills cried.

"You know, this is a very difficult thing to understand, but as much as we might like to, we can't decide who our friends should like," Emma explained.

"Adults can, I bet," Wills said. "But it'll be about a zillion years before I'm an adult," he added bitterly.

"No, adults can't, either," Emma said. She thought about her own friends and about how angry she had felt when Sam went off on a trip with her enemies, and how hurt she was to know that Kurt liked Diana. "It isn't an easy lesson to learn," Emma told Wills.

"I like it better if everyone does what I want them to do," Wills said plaintively.

Emma smiled and hugged the earnest-faced little boy. She understood exactly how he felt.

FIFTEEN

The next morning at breakfast Jane asked Emma to take Katie to her swimming lesson at the club.

"Sure," Emma said, getting up to clear the breakfast dishes. She bit her lower lip anxiously. Well, she was going to have to face Kurt sometime. Might as well get it over with.

Jane caught the look on Emma's face. "Did you and Kurt have a fight or something?" she asked.

"Sort of," Emma admitted.

"Does 'sort of' mean it's temporary?"

Emma sighed. "I don't know. It's really terrible. Are you sure you're interested?"

Katie, Wills, and Ethan stopped midway to the back door, listening attentively.

"If you stay in here, you guys'll have to

load the dishwasher and sweep the floor," Jane warned her kids. They disappeared fast. She got out the broom as Emma started to load the dishwasher. "You can tell me if you want," Jane said, "but you don't have to."

"The short version of a long story is that Kurt went to New York with Diana De Witt," Emma said. "I ran into him there. How's that for rotten luck? Now he and Diana think I went to New York just to spy on them."

"My, my, aren't they full of themselves?" Jane commented as she moved the kitchen chairs to sweep under the table.

"That's what my aunt Liz said," Emma said. "Anyway, before Kurt left, he claimed that he and Diana were just friends. But when I saw them in New York he had his arm around her and she was wearing a T-shirt with a computer image picture of him on it."

"That doesn't sound good," Jane observed.

"She paid for his trip, too," Emma said disgustedly. "After he claimed how much he hated snotty rich girls! *I* could have thrown my money around! *I* could have taken him places and bought him things!"

"But that's not the Kurt you fell in love with, right?" Jane asked.

"Right," Emma answered bitterly. "How can one person be so . . . so two-faced? I mean, who is the real Kurt?"

"Both, probably." Jane put the broom away.

"But that just doesn't make any sense." Emma turned on the dishwasher and wiped viciously at the countertop with a damp sponge. "I could never trust him again, that's for sure."

"That's what he thought about you after you lied to him about being rich," Jane reminded Emma.

"This is different," Emma argued. "He—" The phone rang before she could finish her thought.

"Hewitt residence," Emma said after picking up the phone.

"Hi, it's Carrie! I haven't talked to you in ages!"

"I know," Emma said. "How's life? How's Billy?"

"Great and great." Carrie laughed. "I want to tell you about it in person, though."

"I'm just about to take Katie to her swimming lesson," Emma said.

"Oh, great! I'm taking Chloe, so I'll see you there!" Carrie promised.

"I'll have an ally at the club," Emma told Jane when she hung up the phone. "Carrie's taking Chloe."

"I'll get Katie changed," Jane offered.

Emma ran upstairs and put on her white bathing suit—Kurt's favorite. Ordinarily she didn't wear makeup to the club, but she brushed on some blusher, added mascara to her lashes, and touched her lips with cherry-scented lip gloss. As a final measure she spritzed herself with her favorite French perfume. *Take that, Kurt Ackerman*, she thought.

Katie chatted all the way to the club, but Emma was only half listening. She was giving herself a silent lecture: *You are in control, Emma. Kurt does not control you or your decisions.*

But no matter what she told herself, her heart started to hammer as she and Katie approached the pool and she saw Kurt in the distance. He was talking with Kip, the head lifeguard. Emma couldn't help noticing that his tan was deeper and that his muscles glistened with sunscreen. *So? What's gorgeous?* Emma asked herself. *Gorgeous isn't everything.*

Katie scampered over to the kiddie pool to join her friends. It was hard to believe that she'd absolutely refused to go anywhere near the water until quite recently. Emma found Carrie lying on a chaise longue. To her surprise, Sam was on the chaise next to Carrie's.

"Hi, I didn't expect to see you," Emma said to Sam, choosing the chaise on the other side of Sam.

"The twins are swimming," Sam said, cocking her head in the direction of the main pool. "They got new flowered bikinis, and they had to come and show them off. And speaking of showing off, look at that," Sam said, pointing to Carrie's neck.

Emma leaned close and saw that Carrie was wearing a thin gold chain with a perfect pearl right at the base of her throat. "It's beautiful," Emma said. "Is it new?"

Carrie blushed happily. "It's from Billy."

"Can you believe this girl?" Sam asked, pulling some sunscreen out of her knapsack. "She bags the lead singer of the hottest band around, and he starts buying her presents and writing songs about her! Talk about still waters running deep!"

"He only wrote me one song," Carrie said with a smile.

"Oh, *excusez-moi*," Sam said. "He only wrote one song, which he crooned to you in front of the whole world the other night."

"How was the Flirts concert in Bangor?" Emma asked, pulling her sunglasses on. Even as she spoke with her friends she was hyperaware of Kurt on the other side of the pool.

"Unbelievable," Carrie confessed. "The show ended so late that we ended up spending the night in Bangor."

Sam stopped rubbing sunscreen into her right leg. "Wait a second," she said. "Are you saying you spent the night, or are you saying you Spent The Night?"

"That's one of the things I wanted to tell you guys," Carrie said softly.

"Tell? Tell?" Sam screamed. "You know I live for smut!"

"It was incredibly romantic," Carrie sighed. "First we went to the show, which was just about sold out—"

"She always does this!" Sam groaned.

"Haven't you heard that patience is a virtue?" Emma laughed.

"Please," Sam snorted. "When I rent movies I fast-forward them to the juicy scenes—unless the girl is wearing incredible clothes, of course," she added.

"Fast-forward, please," Emma instructed Carrie.

"So we were lying there afterward in each other's arms, totally happy—" Carrie began.

"Cut, cut!" Sam yelled. "You fast-forwarded too far!"

"Poor Sam," Emma crooned.

"Carrie Alden, did you do it, or didn't you?" Sam demanded.

"Actually, I—" Carrie began eagerly.

"Sammi! Hey, ya'll!" It was the unmistakable voice of Lorell Courtland. She and Diana waved from across the pool and started toward them.

"I suppose I have to be civil," Sam muttered. "I did fly to New York in her father's jet."

"You did?" Carrie asked, looking shocked.

Lorell looked perfect in a pink maillot suit with high-cut legs. Diana wore a red bikini with an underwire bra. How could she be that thin and that busty, Emma wondered with a sigh.

"Shove over, hon," Lorell said to Sam, scooching down on the edge of her chaise longue. Diana sat down next to her.

"Gee, Emma, you just seem to show up everywhere I go," Diana said, batting her eyelashes at Emma.

"Just one of those truly awful coincidences in life, I assure you," Emma said frostily.

Diana raised her eyebrows. "Well, well, the snotty voice of the imperious Emma Cresswell we all know and love comes peeking through, even if what she's saying is a total lie."

"Do you really believe I have nothing better to do with my time than follow you to New York?" Emma asked haughtily.

"You were in New York, too?" Carrie asked Emma. She was completely bewildered.

"Even Sammi knows the truth," Lorell said. "We just laughed and laughed when Diana and Kurt came back to the hotel and told us about seein' you. You need spyin' lessons, Emma!" she laughed. "The spy is not supposed to get caught!"

"I was visiting my aunt," Emma said evenly.

"Puh-leeze!" Diana chortled.

"Isn't Emma just too funny, Sammi?" Lorell asked. She seemed certain that now that "Sammi" had gone with them to New York, she'd be on their side.

"First of all, I never believed that Emma followed you to New York," Sam said. "Second, I never laughed about it. And third, if you call me Sammi one more time I am going to put my fist through your face."

"Well, I never!" Lorell said in a shocked voice. "After we were kind enough to take you on our trip and everything!"

"Trent invited me. You didn't," Sam reminded her.

"It wasn't Trent's jet," Diana pointed out. "You were friendly enough when you wanted something from us, I notice."

"I don't want anything from either of you," Sam insisted. "I was there with Trent."

"Oh, believe me, Sam, I know your type," Lorell said slyly. "You'd have gone with anyone willing to foot the bill." She turned to Diana. "What do they call that, when you trade yourself for money?" she asked, feigning puzzlement.

"Oh, you mean prostitution," Diana said. "Though that's a little too kind. I'd call Sam a plain old gold-digging hooker."

Before Emma could think about what she was doing, she lifted her good hand and slapped Diana's face as hard as she could. Everyone just sat there in shock for a second while Diana held her reddened cheek.

"Why you little bi—" Diana began, reaching for Emma. Sam caught Diana's wrist and held it tight. "I wouldn't do that if I were you," she said in a dark voice. "What I would do is leave. Very, very quickly."

Lorell and Diana both got up. "You haven't heard the last of this," Diana warned Emma. She caught sight of Kurt out of the corner of her eye. "And as for Aquaman, you can have him," she hissed. "Not that he wasn't fun for a little while, but I've met someone with brains and money as well as muscles. That poor-boy routine gets real tired, real fast," she finished viciously.

"In other words, Diana dumped him," Lorell trilled.

"Have fun with your little boy toy," Diana told Emma. "I did." She shook her curls out of her face, and then smiled as if a thought had occurred to her. "Funny, isn't it, Emma, how you turned out just exactly like your mother? Both of you have your own little fortune-hunting boy toys." She looked from Sam to Emma. "Well, you know what they say—birds of a feather . . ."

"Flock together!" Lorell finished for her. "Toodle-oo!" she added, as she and Diana walked away.

"I should have brained her," Sam muttered.

"I am *not* just like my mother," Emma whispered.

"I have a feeling I missed something," Carrie said. "I have a feeling I missed *a lot* of somethings. Can somebody please fill me in?"

But for the moment both Emma and Sam were lost in their own problems, and no one said a word.

SIXTEEN

After a few minutes of stunned silence Emma finally told Carrie everything that had happened.

"So that's the whole ugly story," she concluded.

"Wow, it's amazing that so much happened in just a couple of days," Carrie marveled.

"I never should have gone on that trip," Sam said, shaking her head.

"I thought you said it was fun," Emma said.

"It was—sort of," Sam admitted. "But I had to pretend all the time I was there that I liked the people I was with," she said. "I even had to pretend to myself."

"The three of us should definitely plan a trip to New York sometime," Emma said.

"Oh, I'd love that," Sam said wistfully.

"There's a zillion things I didn't get to do. It would be a riot!"

"Maybe we can do it sooner than you think," Carrie said. Her two friends looked at her. "It's one of the things I wanted to tell you about. Do you remember those photos I took of Graham Perry backstage the night that Flirting with Danger opened for him?"

Emma and Sam nodded.

"Well, I sold them to *Hard Rock News*!"

Emma and Sam both screamed.

"There's more!" Carrie continued eagerly. "They want to commission me to take photographs at the Graham Perry concert next week at Madison Square Garden!"

"Oh, my God, that's fabulous!" Sam screamed.

"Carrie, I'm so happy for you!" Emma cried.

"Graham and Claudia said they'd give me the time off," Carrie continued eagerly. "Claudia's sister and brother-in-law are coming to stay with the kids. Graham said I could travel with them on the band's private plane and everything!"

"I am dying of envy," Sam said.

"Don't die. Just come with me," Carrie said.

"Yeah, right," Sam snorted.

"I'm serious!" Carrie insisted. "That's what I've been trying to tell you! I asked Graham if you guys could come, provided you can get the time off, and he said there's plenty of room in the plane."

"This is fabulous!" Emma cried.

"Carrie, I love you!" Sam threw her arms around Carrie.

"I take it this means you two want to go," Carrie said, laughing.

"What? Party backstage at Madison Square Garden with the top rock star in the world? Travel in his private jet? God, life is a bitch," Sam said.

"I'd love to go, too," Emma said, "if I can get the time off."

"Oh, we absolutely have to," Sam said. "We cannot let work interfere with our lives!"

Emma was so busy laughing at the serious expression on Sam's face that she didn't notice Kurt until he had tapped her on the shoulder.

"Hi," he said.

"Oh, hi." Emma looked over at the kiddie pool. "Class over?"

"Free play for ten minutes. Kip is watching them," Kurt explained. "Could I talk with you a minute?"

"Excuse me," Emma told her friends, then walked with Kurt to the aquatics department office.

Kurt sat down on the edge of his desk. Emma sat in the only chair, her heart was pounding in her chest.

"Now that I actually have you here, I don't know what to say." Kurt laughed nervously.

"Than maybe we should wait until you figure it out," Emma said, getting up to leave.

Kurt held his hand up. "No, don't go, please."

Emma sat back down, and Kurt took a deep breath. "I really care about you, Emma," he began in a low voice.

"You have a very strange way of showing it," Emma said coldly.

Kurt looked down at his hand. "I never really believed that you followed me to New York," he admitted. "I was just . . . Well, you took me by surprise, and I guess I felt defensive."

"So you attacked me," Emma said.

"Yeah," Kurt admitted. "I did."

"What did you have to feel so defensive about? It was just a trip to New York with your good buddy Diana," she said sarcastically.

"That's what it was supposed to be," Kurt said. "Just friends."

"But that's not how it turned out, is it?" Emma shot back. "Did you sleep with her?"

"I don't have to answer that."

"Fine." Emma headed for the door.

"Wait!" Kurt called to her. "Dammit, Emma, you're making this very hard."

Emma turned to face him. "It's not my job to make it easy."

Kurt gulped hard. "Yes, I slept with Diana," he said in a low voice. "I was an idiot. I thought . . . I thought I cared about her. And I thought she cared for me."

Emma was surprised at how much it hurt to have her worst suspicions confirmed. "Kurt, I tried to tell you that Diana doesn't care about anybody but herself."

"I know that now," Kurt admitted. "Everything seemed so easy. There were no big decisions to make . . . "

"Like there are with me," Emma finished for him.

"Yeah," he agreed. "Sex isn't a big deal to

Diana. I didn't have to be Prince Charming or promise to love her forever."

"You didn't have to be perfect," Emma murmured.

"Right," Kurt agreed. "You scared me, Emma. Everything with you was just so . . . so big, so intense."

"So that's why you were willing to throw everything we had away?" Emma cried. "Why didn't you just talk to me?"

"I don't know." Kurt ran his hand across his face. "I guess because I didn't even know myself. And I didn't want to disappoint you."

"So you hurt me," Emma whispered.

"I want you to know I'm not seeing Diana anymore."

"Because she dropped you?" Emma stared at him. "She dropped you, didn't she?"

Kurt nodded.

"Would you still be with her if she hadn't?" Emma asked.

"I don't know. I like to think I wouldn't."

"I like to think that, too," Emma said, gulping hard.

Kurt reached out and stroked her hair. "Emma, you're the best thing that's ever happened to me. I'd give anything to be able to undo all the stupid things I did, to make it up to you somehow."

"But you can't undo them," Emma said sadly, "any more than I can."

"So . . . so what does that mean?" Kurt faltered. There was fear etched on his face.

Emma bit her lip. "I needed you to be perfect, and so in my mind I made you into this perfect person," she said softly. "That part is my fault, and it wasn't fair. You are who you are, and I can't expect you to be the person I want you to be." She looked deep into Kurt's eyes. It was so hard to say what she needed to say. "Maybe you're not ready for the kind of relationship I want. I don't know . . . Maybe I'm not ready for it, either. But I do know that if you could do the things you did, then you aren't the guy I want to be with."

"I can change," Kurt protested.

"It's too late," Emma said quietly. "I'd always resent you for what you did, and it would always get in the way."

"Does 'always' mean 'forever'?" Kurt asked. There was the glint of tears in his eyes.

"I don't know," Emma told him honestly. "I guess we'll just have to wait and see."

Kurt nodded, gulping hard. A part of Emma wanted nothing more than to throw her arms around him, to tell him how much she loved him, to feel safe and protected and loved once again. She desperately wanted to ignore the awful things he'd said and done, to make excuses for him so that she wouldn't be alone.

But another part of her—the part that was absolutely, positively nothing like her mother—turned away from Kurt and walked out the door.

She straightened her back, held her head high, and walked back to her friends. They were there by the pool, waiting for her.